BEYOND MERMAIDS

Also by David Roper

Watching for Mermaids
Rounding the Bend... The Life and Times of Big Red
Getting the Job You Want... Now!

Beyond MERMAIDS

Life's Tangles, Knots, & Bends

DAVID H. ROPER

COPYRIGHT ©2021 DAVID H. ROPER

All rights reserved.

ISBN: 978-0-9856501-4-8

Points East Publishing, Inc.

for Rosie

CONTENTS

PREFACE, 1

ETHICAL TANGLES, 5
Beyond Mermaids, 7
Unlocking the Guilt, 31
Rot in the Bullshead, 35
A Bumblebee Puts Things in Perspective, 39

ALLURING BENDS, 41
Let the Lower Lights Be Burning, 43
Chang Ho's Most Romantic Adventure, 47
Elsa's Dance Card, 51
Why I Love Russians, 55
Conversations in the Cabin, 59
Frightening Lightning, 63

FRAYED, FROZEN AND BROKEN KNOTS, 67

When the Moment's Right, 69

After Touching Leaves of Three, Don't Go Out to Sea, 73

A Frozen Marriage, 77

When Zeus is Mad, 91

A Love Story and a Ghost Story, 95

Beyond Big Red—Toddy's Story, 99

THE END OF THE LINE, 111

Sit Down, Pop, 113

The Tide Waits for No Man, 119

Seven Blocks of Wood, 123

Tilting at Windmills, 125

Some Old Love Song, 129

Polysulfide, 133

"She is water, powerful enough to drown you, soft enough to cleanse you, deep enough to heal you."

— Adrian Michael

PREFACE

It's tempting to draw out the world you want from a picture. A lot of what we remember is fiction. Maybe.

Here, in the picture of a man and a little boy, is a first look at knots. I remember. No, that's not true. I *think* I remember because of what's in the picture. The picture tells some apparent truths: I was about five years old. That was my dad with me. It must have been around 1955. We were standing on an old wooden pier in Hingham Harbor in Massachusetts. It appears to be early spring. And the knot: it looks to be part splice. And one end is frayed.

One thing is certain: It's a picture of my dad showing me about knots. But from there I can only speculate. I can't remember the circumstance. Maybe we had gone down to look at the water after Easter Sunday dinner. Or maybe to get out of the house due to a fight with one of my older brothers.

It appears there's kindness and attentiveness in the picture, though I don't remember the kindness, or the patience, that the photo seems to indicate. Dad does look patient. I do look attentive. But that photo represents only a moment of time the length of a shutter click, taken then preserved. Good, bad or unpleasant things could have happened right before or after. Perhaps my mother took the photo, having set the scene and the shot in a manner that preserved things the way she wanted to see them, capturing what she hoped for in our relationship. And maybe I lost my attentiveness right after the shot. Or my mother started shivering in the damp March air and hurried us along.

It's nice to believe that image really was what it seemed to convey. And that life went on that way from there.

My dad may have leaned down and handed me the length of rope. Or perhaps I picked up the stray piece and handed it to him. Maybe I asked him how to tie a knot. Or what that knot was. Or maybe he wanted to show me. Perhaps he said that there are all kinds of knots. Perhaps I asked him how many? And why there needed to be so many. Maybe he told me that different knots did different things. Perhaps then I looked up at him and asked, what kinds of things? Good things? Maybe he got thoughtful, perhaps philosophic, and said, well, there are good and bad, or wrong things. To which I may have asked, what wrong things? There are wrong knots, like the granny, and those get too tight sometimes, and then it's a mess, hard to untie them, he may have said. And then, perhaps, he thought of the metaphorical side, but changed the subject. He would have known I was too little for metaphors, and that I wouldn't understand about knotted stomachs, being tied up in knots, undoing Gordian knots, or living a life with frayed ends.

Maybe we went home, bringing that piece of line with us. Perhaps that evening, after supper, instead of telling me a story at bedtime, he showed me how to tie a square knot. Or maybe he helped me make my first bowline, showing the way through an imaginative process: making the loop-like circle be a rabbit hole, telling me how the end of the line is the rabbit, and showing me how the rabbit comes out of the hole and goes around the tree— the other part of the line—and then back down the hole again. And then maybe he showed me how, no matter how hard I pulled on the knot, it could always be undone. Maybe he said that to give me hope. Or simply because it was true for this knot. Maybe there was a lesson there. But it would have been too much for a five-year-old to grasp.

Maybe it was then that he put down the knotted line and began to tell me stories, including the ones about two mermaids named Minnie and Maisie who lived under a pier in Hingham Harbor. In each story either an adult or a child was in danger or in trouble. And in each story they were ultimately rescued by the mermaids. There were happy endings in every episode. Why couldn't life go on like that? Why was life so different, beyond mermaids?

Ethical Tangles

BEYOND MERMAIDS

I
FEAR

It was Grace's idea to get the hotel next to the hospital. Arthur remembered the discussion in their kitchen a couple days before. "You have to report for surgery at 5:30 am, Arthur. 5:30 am! Why in God's name do they have to start so soon! Anyway, we'll be smart and stay right across the street. Imagine if we overslept at home, got caught in that damned Boston traffic, and missed the surgery? Now *that* would be enough to give you your heart attack!" she'd said.

"A couple hundred bucks is a couple hundred bucks," Arthur had mumbled.

She'd looked at him, a knowing smirk on her face. "There you go again! Money." She shook her head. Arthur knew what she was thinking: You always worry about money; you always worry about everything.

As usual, Arthur didn't want an argument. Didn't want conflict. Not ever. For past eleven years, since that day in 1972, he had run from conflict, had sprinted toward harmony, as if death was in close pursuit. And maybe this time it was. So, though he hesitated at first, finally he blurted: "Grace, don't you think this, this heart surgery, is for once something I should worry about?" All he wanted in response was an 'Of course, honey, and you *should* be worried, as am I'. But that never came. I'm not some old guy whose heart has worn out, he thought. I'm only 41. Something's really wrong. Doesn't she know that?

Instead, he got the facts. "Arthur, just the drive into Boston in morning traffic will put you at more risk than the surgery. I even looked it up—your surgery chances, I mean. The facts are overwhelmingly on your side. Here's the deal: only two to three percent of people who undergo this surgery actually *die* as a result of the operation. And at your age—which is a lot younger than I am—your odds are probably better than that. Great odds. No worries."

"Grace, I don't want..."

"Look, I'll show you. Pick a number I'm thinking of, one that's between one and a hundred."

"What?"

"No, really. Pick a number."

"No, Grace. Besides, what if I picked the number you're thinking of? What then? Then I'd have real cause to worry."

"No," she said, shaking her head.

"No?"

"If you picked my number, I wouldn't have told you'd picked it, that's all."

And so, they'd taken the hotel room, safely driving into Boston, parking in the hospital garage, and making the short walk to the hotel. It was a modest hotel that seemed to be mostly for patients and their families. Nice place though, with red couches and a big lobby with a bar at one end. Typically, when in hotels, Arthur loved to find a corner chair or couch in the lobby so he could watch the people milling about while he invariably waited for Grace, who would invariably be at the front desk handling or arguing about the room details. He'd sit and wonder about the people milling about, wonder why they were here and where they were going. He would sometimes study them to try to determine if they were unfearful, or, better yet, happy. As if somehow he could learn their secret of contentment just by looking at them. Arthur felt safe there in the corner, in some way insulated, almost hidden, yet still observing.

After Grace checked in, Arthur picked up their bag and they went to their fourth floor room. As he started to insert the key card into the door slot, Grace said: "I saw on one of those TV investigation shows that some of these hotels will actually store your credit card data right on the key card. Can you imagine! So, don't lose that key." Arthur, whose career was in forensic accounting, knew this was a myth, but he didn't want to start an argument, so he just said okay, then unlocked the door, picked up the suitcase, went in, flicked on a light and walked to the window, sliding the curtains back and staring down at a parking lot below. Grace went right to one of the beds, pulled back the sheets and leaned down to inspect. "I saw on *60 Minutes* that lots of these places don't bother to change the sheets. Can you imagine?" She looked closer, her nose almost onto the sheet. "Anyway, hard to tell." She straightened up, groaning a bit. "Arthur, put our bag on the stand there by the dresser." It was really Grace's bag; they only needed one, mostly for her clothes, she'd said. Arthur had cocked his head in response. It was because, Grace told him, that he'd be in a hospital gown for maybe a week, so he wouldn't be needing street clothes.

"Hospital gown?"

"Yes, and there's a slit down the back of those gowns, so you'll have to get used to the considerable exposure to your south side," she said, chuckling.

"What's the slit for?" Arthur asked, for he'd never been a hospital patient before.

"That's to get at things easily, I guess. Anyway, Bunny Wheeler—who's been in these places so many times what with all those problems of hers—she says when you check into a hospital you should just leave everything behind, including your vanity and ego. Leave them all at the door."

Grace laughed.

"I'm not sure that's funny," Arthur said, straight-faced, cocking his head again, as he grabbed his bad right hand. It was a habit he'd had for years, especially when fearful or upset—and he squeezed it, trying, always in vain, to stimulate the nerves to gain back some of the lost feeling.

Grace ignored his comment. "Oh, and Bunny told me that one time in the hospital she had this obese eighty-year-old roommate who was obsessed with not showing her bare back end when she was walked down the hall by the nurses. She wouldn't leave her hospital room until a nurse agreed to walk right behind her." Grace shook her head and smirked. "I mean, who's going to want to look at something like that, anyway?"

Arthur couldn't picture himself living for a week in a white gown with a slit, though he didn't care about his butt showing, or what would happen to his ego or vanity in the hospital. What he feared were scalpels, blood, and not dying on the table. Grace, despite their years of marriage, didn't know about many of these fears. He kept his worst ones hidden. But when this heart surgery was called for, he'd been so fearful he'd spoken to his personal doctor, a caring, blond-haired woman with a Swedish accent, and asked her if there was some way to calm himself. She told him about a book by an expert in mind-body medicine and recommended he read it or listen to the author's tapes. So that's what Arthur did, taking the tapes in his car to the quietest part of town he could find, a cemetery, and parking by its edge on the ocean. And there he sat and listened, closing his eyes, lowering his head, and trying his best to follow the calm, instructive voice on the tape, trying to practice the techniques, which included taking himself back in his mind to a peaceful place. He found it. At first. But then

flashed another image, this one dark, and he opened his eyes, lifted his head, and looked at the gravestones at water's edge in front of his car. The dark image wouldn't go away. Anxiety grew from his gut, then into his head and finally rushed out through his arms to his fisted hands, which he repeatedly banged on the steering wheel. At last he slumped forward, and was still. There was a tap on his passenger-side window. He hadn't noticed the police car that had pulled up alongside him. Arthur rolled down the window. "You all right there, fella? You okay?" the cop asked.
"Sorry. Yeah, I'm fine, officer," he lied.

* * * * * * * * * *

"Arthur? Arthur? I think we should go," Grace said, picking up her purse as she headed to the hotel room door. "Eat early. You know, so you're all digested before the... Anyway, we'll eat at that place right in the hotel. Looked kinda cute."

It was a small Bavarian-themed restaurant adjacent to the hotel's bar. Two Asian women with three young children were seated at the next table. The children seemed content, coloring on kids' paper placemats. But the younger of the two women was clearly in distress. With her head lowered, eyes down, and her hands crossed over her chest, she prayed aloud:

Lạy Cha chúng con ở trên trời,
chúng con nguyện danh Cha cả sáng, nước Cha trị đến,
ý Cha thể hiện dưới đất cũng như trên trời.

Grace looked over at the women. "People come from all over the world to get help here, I've heard. Bunny Wheeler told me this is a world-class hospital. You know, because of that fact, those odds of yours will be even better, I bet."

"Let's leave out the odds stuff. Please, Grace."

"Well, those Orientals came from far away, I bet, to get those good odds."

"They're Asians. Vietnamese."

"Orientals. That's what I said. And how do you know that, them being Vietnamese and all, for God's sake?"

"They're saying the Lord's Prayer in their language: Vietnamese."

She stared at Arthur. "Jesus, Mary and Joseph, how can you know...?"

"Because I've heard it before, Grace."

"When you were over there?" Grace shook her head. Why don't you tell me these things, Arthur? Talk about it. Get it off your chest."

Arthur looked over at the women and children at the next table, but he saw something else. His mind went back. He couldn't stop it. Never could. He saw two praying mamas with their little kids, standing in muddy water, hanging off a half sunken, bullet-riddled sampan, the little ones clinging to their mamas' shoulders. They were looking up at him, this strange white guy from the other side of the planet. They were staring at this man with the big black gun, staring at him as if to ask: 'Are you our last hope or our worst nightmare in this whole messed-up world?'

The server came by. She was a pretty, blond-haired woman wearing a Bavarian-styled white-smocked peasant-type shirt and black cotton pants. A large splotch of ketchup was on her blouse under her left breast. It caught Arthur's eye; it looked like blood. He wondered if she'd seen it; if not, would some other server or her boss point it out? Or would she go the whole evening and then discover it when she got home, leaving her to wonder how many saw it and were turned off by this unpleasant looking blood-like stain.

She placed a couple menus before them and asked if they wanted anything to drink before ordering. Grace didn't look up at her but kept staring at Arthur. It was awkward. Finally, she looked at the server. "I'll have a gin and tonic," Grace said, before twisting her head, indicating her husband. "He can't have any alcohol. He's having open heart surgery tomorrow."

"Oh. Something else then?" the server asked, looking over at Arthur.

"Water's fine," he said.

The server smiled. "Well, good luck on that tomorrow. I'll be right back with your drinks," she said, turning away.

"You've spilled on your blouse," Grace said pointedly, rapidly lifting her chin toward the departing young woman, as if throwing the words over her shoulder.

The server stopped, looked down, and with her forefinger and thumb pulled out the middle of her blouse to see. "Oh dear," she said, clearly embarrassed, and scurried off.

Arthur looked down also, and shook his head; his immediate thought was: Why speak to her in such an accusatory tone? Why not something like 'Oh dear, something must have gotten on your nice white blouse'. He felt angry at his wife and felt terrible for the young woman. He scowled, opened his cloth napkin, and fiddled with the silverware.

Grace saw this. "Oh, now what?"

"Why'd you tell her that?" he asked. "I mean, in that way?"

"What way?"

Arthur thought of responding but didn't. It just wasn't worth it.

II
FLIGHT

After dinner, Arthur lay in bed listening for Grace's light snoring, hoping she'd fallen asleep. Reflections from car headlights in the late night traffic occasionally danced on the ceiling. He was thinking that he shouldn't have watched that open heart surgery video the other day. Odd that he had, given his fears. But there on the screen had been this kindly-looking doctor sitting at his desk, a plastic heart in his hands, explaining the coronary artery bypass grafting procedure. The doctor, with his Indian accent and self-assured, erudite manner, was calm and matter-of-fact in his delivery, as if giving a passerby some instructions to the hospital parking garage rather than details of how he performed open heart surgery. Perhaps this was why Arthur had kept watching. Yet when the blinking warning about upcoming graphic content had appeared, and the video had flashed to an actual open heart procedure, he'd been surprised that he'd continued to stare at the screen. And there, in living color, was the real surgery on a real person. All Arthur had to do to stop it was one click on his remote. But something seemed to hypnotize him, and he'd stared at each step of the procedure, as if believing that when that snap of a finger came, he would be back to his old self and all would be better. He watched as a vein for grafting was harvested from the patient's leg by inserting what looked like a shish kabob skewer with a hook on one end and sliding it under the skin to capture the blood-filled snake-like vein and pull it out from the open incision farther up the limb. He watched as a scalpel cut open the patient's chest; it was like seeing his wife getting a turkey ready for stuffing. And he watched and listened as an electric saw cut through the sternum, and clamps were placed to keep it separated so that now, down inside this human, he could see the heart, beating away, like a frightened, injured bird caught in the crook of a tree.

Flight

Tomorrow that's supposed to be my heart, he thought. He shook his head. No, he couldn't die. Not yet. Not before he'd made one thing right. Or at least tried. "Nope. Not going to happen," he said aloud, almost loud enough to awaken his wife. He looked over at her. They were in twin beds, as Grace had figured he'd be awake all night and they might rest better sleeping apart. Always practical. So damn practical, Arthur thought. Why not hug? Why not hang on together? Especially at a time like this. It made him think of that Willie Nelson (or was it Dolly Parton?) song,

'Come and lay down by my side
'till the early mornin' light
All I'm takin' is your time
Help me make it through the night

She didn't seem as worried as he. Of course he worried. He always worried. Grace, though, she was practical to a fault. Worrying by itself, she always said, was unproductive. You fixed a problem. You didn't worry about it.

Well, he thought, now *he* must fix things. Or at least resolve them. Before the surgery. Before it goes all wrong. Before his time on earth runs out, and leaves him lying, pitifully, on the table, a mouth-tubed, pried open carcass who never had the chance to make things right. He knew this level of fear; he'd felt it before, and it had beaten him, many years ago, many thousands of miles away. He wasn't going to let it beat him again.

Slowly, quietly, he arose and went to the dresser, pulled out a pen and the pad of hotel stationery from the top drawer, tiptoed into the bathroom, and sat on the toilet, where he wrote this note:

Grace – I'm sorry, but there is something I HAVE TO DO.
Please cancel my surgery. I won't be there.

But I will return. Please don't worry. And DO NOT call the police. — *Arthur*

Then he dressed, grabbed his wallet and car keys, crept past Grace, and left the hotel.

It was 1:30 am. He drove north on I95, his mind fixed on a certain small town on the coast of Maine, and the hope that she'd still be there. And what would she be like? And what would he say? He would tell the truth. No need to prepare for that. Or was there? He was becoming so lost in thought he could barely focus on his driving. Images washed in, as if sliding through the windshield on the light beams of oncoming cars: people—Hayes, Skid, Sunburn, Howard, and of course Moose; water—turning from aqua-clear to light chocolate brown as they slipped from the South China Sea into the river; sounds—the rumble of the twin GM 12V71s inside their fifty-foot Swift Boat, and then that clatter, that racket of the .50 caliber machine guns and the 81mm mortar. Again, the people. His crew. They were kids, really—kids hungry for action and feeling empowered; kids somehow awarded the keys to a high speed aluminum Swift Boat hull equipped with a virtual arsenal of firepower. Invincible youth. Kids in a candy store. Kids who should have agreed to follow strict base orders to never go into the rivers, but instead hang offshore and patrol back and forth for trawlers loaded with ammunition for the Viet Cong. Kids who then became antsy after seeing nothing, day after day. Kids finally lured by the intrigue of that Bo De river mouth. What's in there? "Come on, Skipper," they'd said to him. "Let's find out. Fuck the base's orders." Kids. Opening Pandora's Box.

First light came as Arthur, now in Maine, wound through smaller and smaller secondary roads, past tidal inlets that flooded him with the familiar smell of pines and the sea. When he got to the cove he stopped, got out, and sat by the shore. There was a pretty wooden sloop at anchor amidst the lobster boat fleet. It was one not unlike his own. He wondered if the owners were aboard, still sleeping, or beginning to arise from a blissful night. A light breeze came with the dawn, and with it the smell of coffee and bacon, eclipsing the cove's natural scent. He knew it came from the small coffee shop near the wharf upwind of him. He knew this because of everything he'd been told, hour after hour, on those long, oddly chilly nights off that river mouth on the other side of the world so many years ago. He turned and headed to the café, but the closed sign on the door told him it was still too early—it was around 4:30 a.m.—so he decided to drive around for a while. Eventually he parked down the road and just sat in the car before dozing off.

III
ROSIE

Rosie's first thought when she awakened was about the tide. Her mom had told her that this would be an extreme low-tide morning as it was the day after the full moon. But Rosie knew that already. For a young girl, Rosie knew more about the tides than most adults. When she was *really* little, Poppy, her grandfather and a lobsterman, told her bits and pieces. They were small pieces, practical ones and suitable for a young child to absorb, though some didn't make sense to her. One morning when the boat was tied up at the wharf her grandfather told her about the tide's six-hour-in, six-hour-out cycles. When he had finished, she put down one of the yellow-and-blue lobster buoys, cocked her head, put her hands on her hips, and asked him why that was so. Poppy wasn't sure, so he used his standard answer.

"It's just the way it is, Rosie."

That wasn't enough for her. "But why would the tide bother to waste all that energy to come all the way in, and then just give up and go all the way out?" she asked.

Several years later, at ten years old, Rosie began to read books about tides. "Did you know," she said one evening at dinner, "the tide is actually a really large and really long wave that travels around the world at 450 miles per hour! It has no beginning and no end. And its energy going in and out isn't wasted because humans use that energy! But you guys know that, right?"

Her mom and Poppy smiled as if they did, then rose to clear the dishes. But Rosie wasn't done. She put her elbows on the table, fists under her chin, narrowed her eyes, and looked at them. "Well, I bet you didn't know this: tides create friction by rubbing against the ocean floor, and this is like a giant brake on the earth's rotation."

Poppy put down his coffee mug and looked at his granddaughter. "Refresh my memory, Pumpkin: are you a ten-year-old elementary school student or a really, really small graduate student?"

"Hahaha! It's the truth, Poppy. But here's what's the coolest: because of this friction, by a teeny amount each day, the earth is turning slower and the days are growing longer. It's all *because* of the tide!"

"I probably knew that, too," Poppy said. Rosie's mom smirked and rolled her eyes.

—∞—

The extreme low tide that morning meant a few more precious minutes of sleep for most everyone in Haskell's Cove. The lobstermen would go out a bit later to pull their traps because most of the skiffs that took them out to their boats would still be grounded out at the end of their outhaul lines. That meant the men would arrive at the Coffee Pot Café a little later as well; and that meant Rosie had a few more minutes of sleep. She tried to take it while Jenipurr, her orange tabby cat, gazed down at her, patiently waiting for breakfast. Rosie knew she was there—she could hear the purring—but pretended to be asleep, trying to buy some time. Soon the cat started losing patience, moving closer and closer to Rosie's face, then tentatively placing a paw on Rosie's nose. She tried this several times. When that didn't work, she moved to plan B: the tissue box on the bed table. With the claws of her right front paw she began pulling out one tissue at a time and dropping each on Rosie's nose.

"Okay, cool it with the tissues, Jen. I'm getting up." Just Rosie's voice made Jenipurr stop, jump off the bed, and make a beeline for her bowl in the kitchen.

Later, as she headed back to her bedroom from the kitchen, Rosie pulled off her Garfield nightshirt (*I Work Hard So My Cat Can Have A Better Life*). She made her usual early morning peek out the window, both to check out the day and to make sure no customers or any delivery folks were already waiting outside the café. The sheer white cotton curtains moved in the whisper of a sea breeze. As she peeked out, she took a breath through her nose as if to confirm the low tide she could already see. Then she did a quick scan of the area below the apartment, which was above the café.

She almost didn't see him. He was standing by the water's edge, nearly out of her view, a stranger staring out at the cove. The first light of day wasn't intense enough to fully define him; he was almost a shadow, as if stuck between night and day. Seems very early for someone to be here, Rosie thought. Especially weird to see a car with Massachusetts plates.

Rosie shrugged.

She could hear the shower running and padded down the hall to the bathroom. "I'm up, Ma," she said, opening the door a crack; creeping tendrils of steam, like that persistent Haskell's Cove fog, slipped out, her mom's voice following. "I'll be down in fifteen, Sweetie."

"I'll start the Bunn and fryolator. No worries, Ma."

―∞―

It was 7 a.m. when Arthur awakened. His neck was stiff. He was surprised he had dozed for so long. He returned to the café, parking amidst the Maine-plated, trap-laden pickups. The earlier crowd of lobstermen who habituated the booths and counter was dwindling; many were finishing up, starting to head out to haul traps. Arthur nodded, half smiled, and held open the café's well-worn blue screen door as a husky, gray-bearded man exited. Once inside, it didn't feel right for Arthur to take one of the stools at the counter; it drew too much attention and somehow seemed reserved for locals. So, even though he was alone, he sat in one of the two empty booths by a window. The booth faced the counter and partly overlooked the wharf. He noticed small pictures of individuals in a hodgepodge of frames on the wall behind the counter. He was staring at them when an energetic young girl in jeans and holding a coffee pot came over. She was wearing a blue-hooded sweatshirt with Dr. Seuss' *Cat in the Hat* emblazoned in the center. She poured him coffee without asking, then gave him a second glance.

"Do you work here? I mean, you must be only . . ." Arthur began.

"I'm going on eleven," she said before he could finish. "My mom's the owner. So it's okay." She looked at him quizzically. "Was that you I saw out front a couple of hours ago?" she asked. "You're not some food inspector or something?"

Arthur shook his head. "But that was probably me earlier," he said, looking up at her. He didn't want to stare, but he was curious about her sweatshirt. The Cat in the Hat artwork was easy to see, but the smaller sub-text print he couldn't make out unless he leaned in toward her and squinted. He didn't dare do that, felt it would be rude, so he let it go.

"Anyway, what would you like?" she asked, handing him a well-worn menu.

"Just coffee is fine," he said.

She looked at him—a man who appeared pale, blank, wooden—and she was concerned.

When she left, Arthur sat for some time, as if in a trance, staring out the window at the wharf as the café crowd thinned to just a few customers. Occasionally, the young girl returned to see if he wanted to order. Arthur just shook his head absently.

"You're from away, I guess?" she asked finally, as she topped up his coffee.

"Yes."

"You need anything else? Anything at all?"

He shook his head again.

A little later, when the place was empty, she came by and stood by the edge of his booth.

"You okay then, mister? I mean, none of my business, but it seems like..."

His anxiety made him want to deflect his reason for being there, so he looked up quickly and asked, "So, those folks on the wall?"

"People who died. Favorite customers," she said, looking over her shoulder at the pictures.

He looked back at her and saw two moist eyes. "Actually, one is my dad, the other is my grandpa, Poppy," she said.

"Sorry. You want to sit down?"

She half sat on the edge of the seat opposite him, then shook her head, wiped her nose. She looked at Arthur, then back at the picture. "Poppy, he was...," she started to say but didn't finish. When she turned to him again, Arthur saw something different in her face, an odd blend of sadness, anger, and perhaps a little embarrassment at having confided in a stranger. "Stubborn, stubborn, stubborn," she continued. "Had a heart attack. He called it his 'event'. Like it was something to celebrate, something that happened and then would just fade away. I told him to take it easy... *please*. But who listens to a kid?"

"You two were close, huh?"

"We hung out together *all* the time. I pulled traps with him starting since I was seven." She looked back at the wall. "Then he's gone. Just gone. Didn't have to happen."

Time stood still. As the sunlight of that new day came into the café's easterly window and drove away the shadows, Arthur stared at her. There was something about this young girl that was so earnest, so deliberate, so unusual for her age. Something about her disarmed him, opened him up, vented his conscience.

"I'm supposed to be in Boston in heart surgery right *now*," he blurted. "I ran away. Left to come here."

Rosie gave him a perplexed look. "Why would you *do* that?" she asked. She scowled at him, then turned and pointed at her grandfather on the wall. "He ran, too, you know. Out on his lobster boat when he knew better. And now look." She shook her head. "No, Mister, if you don't do this surgery, everybody loses."

"I came here first to give your mom something. And I guess to confess something," he said somberly, looking down at his coffee cup. "In case I didn't make it through this heart surgery." Arthur looked toward the kitchen. "Your mom's Lily, right?"

"You know my mom?"

Arthur looked up and looked her straight in the eye, something he'd never been good at. "You're Rosie, aren't you?"

She looked at him—incredulous, perplexed, a bit fearful.

"I knew your dad." He looked up to the pictures behind the counter "I see him, too, up there on the wall. And I know you never got to know him. And, well, that's because of me."

Rosie stood, confused. Moved a few steps back. Stopped. "You need to talk to Ma," she said, and darted into the kitchen, leaving the coffee pot on the table.

When Lily came out of the kitchen, untying her apron, he saw the resemblance to the dog-eared photo of her that Moose had shown him when they were in Vietnam eleven years ago. He remembered the curly brown hair, the eager, yearning eyes, the small fragile smile. Arthur stood, his hands folded in front of him, as if in supplication. Lily was silent and stared blankly at him as he slowly reached into his pocket and handed her a gold bracelet. She stared at it in silence for a few moments, then said, more to the bracelet than to Arthur, "Oh my God. This is Marty's. I gave it to him." She rubbed it lovingly between her thumb and forefinger, then took a step toward Arthur, who backed up against the side of the booth.

"Moose—I mean Marty; we called him Moose—he wanted me to give it to you if anything happened to him," Arthur said.

She was perplexed at first, until anger crept into her face. "So, it took you eleven years?"

"I...I put it away. Too much..." Arthur struggled, his mind trying in vain to push out the words 'pain' and 'cowardice'. Instead, he looked down at his feet. "I'm sorry. So sorry," he said finally.

Lily and Rosie stared at him. A couple of gulls landed on the railing just outside the café's picture window and began squawking and fighting over a half-eaten crab. Arthur looked up and over at the birds, and then back at Lily.

"Look, I know you know what happened to him. It's just that... well, it's just that it wasn't me. I ducked down. Moose didn't. And then, after that..." Arthur looked away again, out the café's window. One of the gulls had taken control of the half-eaten crab; the other stood back, looking tentative. "It's just that after that there hasn't been much holding me together," he said.

"Holding *you* together? What about us?" Lily said, looking over at Rosie. "What did we have holding *us* together? You ever wonder about that? Wonder what *that's* like?—having a fiancé on the other side of the world, a baby growing inside you, growing along with all those dreams of having a little family. And then..." She paused, seething now, glaring at Arthur. Then, with more sadness than anger, she said, "You know what it's like holding a newborn when you know she'll never get to meet her father? Ever." She looked over at her daughter. "So, what'd we have to remember him by? Nothing. Nothing but some boilerplate military letter from some bureaucrat in Washington. And now *you* come along." Lily turned to go back to the kitchen, took a few steps, stopped and turned back to Arthur. "Maybe you want to tell us he was a hero. Well, you're eleven years late. And that ain't heroic. Mister, I think you should get out of my café. Go home to your own family."

Arthur turned, opened the café's blue screen door and walked to his car. He got in and sat there, paralyzed, his forehead resting on the steering wheel. It's not enough, he thought. No, it's even worse. I've just made everything even worse. Startled by a tap on his driver-side window, he lifted his head and turned. A blue sweatshirt was inches away, so close he could only see the red-and-white-striped hat, the red bow tie, the goofy grin of The Cat in the Hat, and what was written below:

> *"To the world you may be one person.*
> *But to one person you may be the world."* — Dr. Seuss

Arthur lowered the window.

"I want to hear about my dad," Rosie said. She looked over her shoulder at the café, then turned her head toward the sea and gestured. "Down on the wharf. We can go there. Talk."

They sat across from one another at a weathered picnic table set between blue plastic bait barrels. In the distance Arthur could hear the throaty, revving engine of what must have been a lobster boat. Rosie put her hands together under her chin and leaned forward on her elbows. He looked at her freckled nose, her wavy auburn hair, and those inquisitive hazel eyes. If he had a daughter, she'd be like this, he thought. If only his wife had wanted a daughter. Or any children at all. Well . . .

"Moose? That's what you called him?" she began. It was as if she knew the perfect way to get Arthur talking. And he began. He told her how he and Moose had leveraged their boating experience to sign up for the Swift Boats that patrolled the Vietnam coast during the Vietnam War. "We had no idea what we were getting into. Your dad thought it would be cool to drive those hot boats. And I thought . . . well, I just figured it would be a whole lot different than it was. Anyway, we first met in a place called Cam Ranh Bay, then flew south to this place called Cat Lo. We talked a lot on the way. He'd just learned your mom was pregnant with you.

God, I still remember his excitement, him saying over and over: It's gonna be a little girl. I just know it. It's gonna be a little girl named Rosie. Ain't that the best damn name?"

Arthur looked down at the rough red wood of the picnic table, tightened his lips, tried to compose himself. Then he looked up; Rosie was crying.

They sat in silence. Rosie wiped the sleeve of her sweatshirt across her eyes and nose. "I wondered," she said finally, "back in the café... how you knew my name?"

"Your dad told me that's the name he wanted way back then... you just never forget those kinds of things. And then, in the café this morning, I don't know how, but somehow, I knew it had to be you. Anyway, while we were in Vietnam, the subject of Maine came up and then boats. Your dad was, of course, on the commercial lobster boat side; me, well I grew up cruising the coast of Maine on a sailboat." Arthur gave a slight smile, his first in a couple of days. "He kidded me, you know, about this 'yachtie' stuff: pink shorts with lobsters on them, boat shoes, and how lobstermen are out there working their butts off and we're—how'd he put it?—drifting along and sipping rosé."

She smiled. "From everything I heard from Ma and folks, that sounds like him," she said.

"Well, we got close. Maybe it was because of boats, or the coast of Maine, but I think it was more. We were so different: me being older, an officer and all, and Moose being an enlisted guy. But we needed each other. On the Swift Boat we were like a family." Arthur looked out at the little pine tree-covered islands that dotted the cove's opening. He pinched his nose and turned his watering eyes away. The fighting gulls had returned to the wharf. Mean, greedy bastards, he thought. But beautiful just the same.

What happens to people? he thought. Sailing peacefully in a beautiful place. Or pulling traps from the sea to feed the family. Why can't it go on like that?

"Was he afraid?" Rosie asked.

Arthur looked back at her. "Maybe. But he never showed it."

"Ma says he was the kind of man who never backed down from anything. She told me once she got messed with by a bunch of guys in a Portland bar back when she was first engaged to my dad. She was able to run out, get away, before anything worse happened. Then she went over to his apartment and told him about it. Just let it be, she told him, nothing really bad happened. Which bar? he asked. That was all. And he just got in his truck and drove away—didn't even ask her for a description of who they were. Just went into the place. And you know what he did? He grabbed the first person he saw, lifted him by the shirt collar, set him on the bar, and said, 'Point to the guys that messed with Lily Brown. Right now, or I'm going to rip your eyeballs out!' Yup, that's what he said. And the guy pointed. And four guys ran for the door." Rosie paused, looked out at the cove, then lifted her head a bit and looked beyond. She seemed so proud. Proud of someone she'd never even met. Then, without looking at Arthur, she asked, "So what happened over there?"

What happened? What happened? He must have replayed it in his head ten thousand times. He grabbed his bad right hand and squeezed it.

"We were supposed to patrol along the coast but not go into the rivers because of ambushes. So, we just patrolled by the river mouth, back and forth, day after day, seeing nothing. The guys got bored. Wanted some action. Wanted to see what was in there behind all those trees. We all did, I guess." Arthur looked down. "They talked me into it." He shook his head. "I was an idiot to go in." With his good hand he picked at the splintered end of one of the table's rotted planks, then smoothed it down with his thumb. "Anyway, when we entered the river, Moose and I were both in the wheelhouse. Your dad was at the wheel, and I was standing next to him. The rest of the crew was on deck. Then it happened: all chaos and noise and orange flashes coming from the trees on the riverbank." Rosie looked at him, wide-eyed. This is it, Arthur thought, don't run, get it out. "I dove under the chart table, covered my head with my hands and . . . well, I just stayed down there. You dad stayed standing, a huge target, while steering a zigzag course, trying to dodge bullets."

"But he didn't," Rosie said.

"Didn't?"

"Dodge them all."

"No."

"Ma would say he wouldn't have ducked down, no matter what. Ma would say that he wasn't a duck-down kind of guy," Rosie said.

Arthur was having a tough time fighting back tears.

Rosie came around and sat with him on his side of the bench. "And what if you *hadn't* ducked down. What then? Then you'd *both* have been shot. Who's driving the boat then? And what happens to the rest of the crew after that?"

"I don't know. I just don't know."

"You didn't do the shooting. You did the ducking. And my dad stood and steered. That's who he was."

Arthur turned to her; he'd never seen so much simple sincerity in one face, never felt something as true as what she'd said. A hundred hours spent paying therapists to find his way out of hell, and now along comes this eleven-year-old, the very daughter of the man at the core of it all, and points the way. He looked over at her, wanted to hug her, but she was gazing at something in the cove.

"Those lobster buoys," she said. "When I was real little, lobstering with my Grandpa Poppy, he told me that maybe someday we'd pull up a trap with a mermaid in it." Rosie smiled. A very soft, thoughtful smile. "Funny, but I never wished for a mermaid."

"No?"

"No, I wanted a merman. I wanted to pull up a dad."

There was an awkward silence. A long silence. A sea breeze began to build, adding a chill to the summer air. Arthur looked at her as she flipped up the hood of her sweatshirt. Finally, he said something he'd been thinking of saying all morning. He looked right at her sweatshirt. "You know, Rosie, *I'm* a big Dr. Seuss fan."

She turned, amazed.

"No! Oh, my gosh. Really?" She looked down at the front of her sweatshirt, as if talking to the Cat in the Hat. "Wow, that's weird."

"'We are all a little weird, and life's a little weird,'" Arthur said.

"*That's* from Dr. Seuss," Rosie said confidently. Then she stood and brushed off the seat of her pants. "Well, I have to get back to help Ma prep for lunch," she said. "But don't worry about Ma; she'll come around."

As Rosie began to walk away, Arthur held his breath, afraid to break this delicate thread that now hung in the air, this thread that had just connected them. "I have something for you. Something special," he blurted.

Rosie stopped and turned.

"I was given it when I was your age. A signed copy. It's *How the Grinch Stole Christmas!* Perhaps, well, if it's okay with your mom, I could come back again and bring it to you." Arthur took a breath. Held it.

She beamed, then cocked her head and put on a serious look. "Okay. But first you *have* to get your heart fixed," she said, before turning her gaze back to the lobster buoys out in the cove. Then she spoke again, this time very softly into the light summer breeze, which carried her words back to Arthur. "I bet my dad would have wanted you to," he heard her say.

Arthur let go of his bad right hand. He exhaled deeply, and glanced at Rosie as she headed up the path to the café. Then he looked up at the bright blue Maine sky and smiled.

UNLOCKING THE GUILT

When the boats were all put away for the winter, and before the crocuses broke through to signal the coming of spring, the grandfather decided to build a grandfather clock. "An old-style clock with a slow swinging pendulum just seems appropriate, given where your mother and I are in life," he'd said to his sons. He'd built wooden boats before and still had his tidy workshop in the basement, so the project began easily and progressed well. It was a long, cold and snowy winter, and the grandfather clock maker was home a lot; besides, he had to tend to his ailing wife. He looked forward to the clock work and to the occasional visits from his grandchildren. His youngest, at seven and eight, came by the most, as they loved the train set he had built in his sprawling basement. The landscape mimicked the town they lived in. The yacht clubs were there; their dad's office building was there; even the grandfather's house was represented. And, of course, there was the harbor. The littlest grandchild was a girl of seven. Typical for her age, she lived through her fantasies, so this fit right in (though the world of Cinderella was always her favorite).

When the clock was finished and grandfather had invited them to see it finally working, she saw the key for the first time. The tall clock loomed over the little seven-year-old and her eight-year-old brother, and seemed to speak to them through the tick tock of its giant pendulum, which swung from its place behind the mahogany door in the clock's front. But what caught her attention was the big brass key in the front. Grandfather turned the key and the door opened; behind was the swinging pendulum. It was magical.

A couple of weeks passed. On their next visit to the clock, Grandfather knelt in front of the children and told them something had disappeared and now he couldn't open his clock to wind it. The key was gone! He asked if they would help him look for it. He would give a dollar to anyone who found it. The two children searched everywhere—under couches and behind tables—to no avail.

Months went by; seasons passed. A new year came. The little girl and her brother went with their parents to a faraway place called Lake Powell in Utah. They stayed in a small hotel in a spot called Wahweep, where they looked out on the mystical lake with its countless side canyons, inlets and coves sheltering Indian ruins and natural wonders. The little girl had never seen a world like this. But there was more. The next day, on a small tour boat, they journeyed 55 miles through sandstone canyons hundreds of feet high, set amidst this mysterious lake world, which came from the damming of the Colorado River. They arrived at a place called Rainbow Bridge. There was a dock just big enough for the cruise boat to tie up. And there before them it loomed. The little girl looked up at the largest natural bridge in the world, higher than the nation's Capitol Building and nearly the length of a football field. Water flowing from Navajo Mountain had eroded the river's sandstone banks. The result? The lofty 290-foot-tall and 270-foot-wide arch that towered above her. The little girl listened intently as the captain told them that Rainbow Bridge was considered sacred by the Navajo culture as a symbol of the gods responsible for creating clouds, rainbows and rain—the essence of life in the desert. Would the passengers like to take this rare opportunity to walk up to and even under the bridge, the captain asked. Everyone did.

Unlocking the Guilt

Everyone except this one little girl with the yellow fanny pack and the Cinderella lunch box. She wanted to stay. So she, her father and the captain remained. Her father, who used to drive a cruise boat himself, engaged the captain, and they chatted away about the area and tour boats while they watched the departed tourists climbing to the top of the great Rainbow Bridge.

"Just a minute; please don't interrupt," the dad said as his little girl pulled on his jacket. The pulling stopped. But then there was another tug. It wasn't like her; she was a well-mannered seven-year-old. And so, excusing himself from the captain, he turned to his wide-eyed daughter, whose face held a look that was both entranced and guilt-ridden at the same time. In her hand she held a key—a big brass key. The one from her grandfather's clock.

"What's that?"

"It's the key. The key to Grampy's clock."

"What? I'm confused. When and where did you ever find it, Sweetie?"

"I didn't find it. I took it. I've been keeping it in my fanny pack since last year." Her lip began to quiver, and big tears formed. "I was scared to tell Grampy. And I thought it was magic and could unlock anything."

Lost for words, the dad scratched his head. "But why now? Why here?"

The little girl looked up at the looming arch ahead of them and the sacred Indian landscape.

"This seemed like a good place to tell somebody," she said.

ROT IN THE BULLSHEAD

They owned a small inn on the coast of Maine, and they came in earnest down to Marblehead, Massachusetts, to view our robin's egg blue 19′ Corinthian sloop, which my growing family had outgrown. A young couple as sweet as our little sailboat, though a bit naïve about sailing, they had a good natural eye for a seaworthy, well-designed craft. With a very deep cockpit, full keel, and small cabin, *Windmill* had served us well and had been perfect for our sailing lives while our two kids grew from babies to four- and five-year-olds. She sat in our driveway on a trailer, waiting for another season of sailing. Nicky, our precocious five-year-old, was all excited that chilly morning as we awaited the prospective buyers. He wanted to help me sell the boat. He held up his open but still tiny right hand. "Daddy, I have five years at sea on *Windmill*, just like you. They will want to talk to me too, I bet." It was true; he and I had done everything together on that little boat. Like a small, loyal and inquisitive puppy, Nicky had always been right there beside me and, unbeknownst to me, he had absorbed EVERYTHING about the boat. "Daddy, I can show them around the cabinet (his word for the tiny crawl-space cabin); and I can show them how the head works, and how to fix it." He took a breath and continued, his mind obviously spinning with all he knew. "And all the other stuff: how the motor works, how these crankers (Nicky's word for winches) pull in the sail, and where we keep the anchor rope."

He really does know a lot, I thought to myself. Maybe too much; I began to get nervous, especially about some bad areas in the cockpit bulkhead. "Nicky, maybe Daddy should do the adult talking about why they would like to buy the boat," I ventured. He gave me a quizzical look and then that cute, exaggerated double-shoulder 'whatever' shrug that five-year-olds are known for. "I'll signal you when it's your turn to talk, okay? You do want to sell *Windmill* so we can get that Cape Dory with the bigger sleeping cabinet, right?" Then I quickly tried to distract him before he could counter (for even at five his mental alacrity was beginning to eclipse mine). "And you can help me set up the ladder so we can all climb right aboard when they arrive," I said.

When the young couple did arrive, we exchanged pleasantries about their drive from Maine, and the history of our town of Marblehead. All the while Nicky waited patiently, seemingly adhering to my instructions. But then talk turned to discussing the boat, and this was when I first met the salesman inside my young son. As Arthur Miller wrote in his famous play: "For a salesman, there is no rock bottom to life. He's a man way out there in the blue, riding on a smile and a shoeshine."

Nicky Roper, the salesman, took over.

"Let's start with the trailer," he said with a confident smile, and he crouched his forty-eight-inch frame by the right front tire of the tandem trailer. "Don't let this rust worry you," he said, tapping the frame of the trailer. "That's normal cause it gets wet all the time." Then he moved to one of the tires. "You need to check here, to look for loose bears," he said. We all smiled.

"Bearings, Nicky," I corrected.

"Yes, bearings," he said, self-correcting with a somehow erudite tone.

"Nicky, let's show them the cockpit," I suggested. We all climbed the ladder.

Rot in the Bullshead

"Watch your step," Nicky said to the young wife. Once safe in the cockpit, the pitch continued. He explained about the outboard motor well, where the choke was on the outboard, how the gas can needed to be vented, and how you could take the motor out of the well and put it under the seat for less drag when sailing. "Even Grampy likes this feature," he said, "and he's the Cow Manure at a yacht club even."

"It's 'Commodore', Nicky," I corrected.

"Yes, well, Commodore."

Then, with great pride, he showed them the small mahogany switch panel box I made for the cabin and told how most Corinthians didn't have such cool shiny (read: varnished) wood in the cabin.

Then he got to the toilet, which was a marine head—this was before the days of holding tank requirements—that sat under the little v-berth. "Excuse me," he said to the couple as he squeezed by them into the cabin. Taking a hammer out of the tool bin, he got down on his knees in front of the main thru-hull for the head. "This can be stuck," he said. "But you just crawl down like me, get way under here, and tap it with this hammer. On hot days, Dad says some swears while he does this, but you might not want to do that."

And so, the sales process continued. I think if Nicky himself were for sale and not *Windmill*, the closing would have been quicker. But we were getting there.

The young husband turned his attention to me. "Are there any areas we should be concerned about then?" he asked.

I gave this a false ponder. Or was it? This was not a structural issue. It wasn't a safety issue. And it could be fixed. It was just the connotation of one particular word that concerned me. "Well, I don't..." I began to say.

"You should tell them about the rot, Daddy."

"Well, Nicky, I was just getting to that."

He got down on his little knees again and pointed to the base of the cabin bulkhead where it met the cockpit floor.

He looked back at the couple and smiled self-confidently at his ability to enlighten them with his esoteric knowledge of such a hidden flaw.

"That's rot in the bullshead," he said with a now serious look.

Yes, rot in the bullshead. I should have spoken of that.

It was almost a deal breaker.

A BUMBLEBEE PUTS THINGS IN PERSPECTIVE

I will arise and go now, and go to Innisfree,
And a small cabin build there, of clay and wattles made:
Nine bean-rows will I have there, a hive for the honey-bee;
And live alone in the bee-loud glade.

William Butler Yeats

I've always liked bumblebees, but that Sunday morning my mind was elsewhere when I spied one on deck, upside down and caught under the jib sheet of my sailboat. I wasn't in a compassionate mood.

"Good luck, dude, but I have my own problems," I said dismissively as I climbed aboard to try once again to fix a broken engine. In hindsight, perhaps I might have jumped to his assistance if I'd known more about bumblebees at the time: that they use a combination of color and spatial relationships to learn from which flowers to forage; that around one third of human food requires bee pollination; that the bee is a Spirit Animal and nature's reminder that it's possible to be yourself while also doing good for the world.

But instead I went about my business with the engine problem until, a couple hours later, I gave up, grumpier than ever.

Back in the dinghy, still alongside and about to row off, I glanced over at the still-trapped bumblebee. It seemed as if the little guy was looking at me. I flashed on a book on compassion that I'd been reading, how science was proving that compassionate people were happier people. So why not show compassion, even to a bumblebee? What good could possibly come from leaving him there? I reached up to free the little guy by flicking him out from his trapped position under the jib sheet. But he stuck like glue to my finger, as if clinging to me for dear life. My immediate reaction was to shake him off. As I did so he shot up in the air and landed in the water behind me. I shook my head, pushed off, and started rowing for the dock, looking back at him. He was upside down again, trying to turn over, but his little wings weren't up to the task. A few strokes later I stopped. "You know, you're not much of a human," I said aloud to myself. "You've got yourself a First World problem, Dave: Your yacht's motor won't run right, for God's sake. Poor Dave. But this guy's DROWNING. And you're just rowing away."

So I turned around, scooped up the bumblebee with the blade of my oar, and slid him off the oar onto the cushion on the stern seat. As I continued my row to shore, I watched him shake himself dry in the sun and then use his wings to finally turn himself over. I rowed another fifty yards, watching him watch me as he continued to dry off on the cushion.

And then he flew off, headed to shore. But he soon turned back my way, zooming down low over my head, so close I could hear his buzz, a bee-loud buzz. Or was it just a buzz? Maybe it was his way of saying thanks. Maybe it was his way of reminding me that, big or small, we're all in this world together.

Alluring Bends

LET THE LOWER LIGHTS BE BURNING
LABOR DAY MAGIC, 1990

Let the lower lights be burning! Send a gleam across the wave!
Eager eyes are watching, longing, for the lights, along the shore.
Trim your feeble lamp, my brother, some poor sailor tempest tossed,
Trying now to make the harbor, in the darkness may be lost.
Philip P. Bliss

He was up before the rest of the family that first morning of our stay in the log cabin that faced northeast and clung to the ledges on this magical island in Salem Sound. He and his sister slept on the two couches in the rustic living room with its iron wood stove and small drop-leaf table by the four windows; open wide, they beckoned the sounds and smells brought up from the crashing northeast swell. Who knows how well the children slept that night in their strange and wondrous new surroundings, as all night, with perfect regularity, the swath of the lighthouse's broad beam invaded the living room and then departed just as suddenly, as if some flashlight-wielding giant was searching, searching, searching for a little boy and a little girl. The giant seemed even closer when the noise came, in the days to follow, as the fog rolled in: BOOWAAAAAH, BOOWAAAAAH, BOOWAAAAAH came the great lighthouse's moan.

But there was no fog that first night, and the next day dawned bright and clear as I awoke from a little boy's excited tug on my arm. "Dad, Dad, Mom, Mom, get up, get up. Get up and see the big orange monster. It is coming out of the sea," five-year-old Nicky said. And there it was, a beautiful sun rising out of the sea from the east. Only the top half was showing as I sat up and looked out the window of the tiny bedroom where Mary Kay and I slept.

"Get your little sister up to see it too," said my immediately bright-eyed wife.

"Yikes," I said, "it's getting bigger, coming our way. Maybe we should make a run for it, hide behind the lighthouse." Instead, Nicky stared, mesmerized for a few moments, as we watched the sun emerge from the sea. Then he cocked his head and gave me that confident, knowing look of a soon-to-be kindergartener.

"Dad, I think what it is, well, it's only the sun, but it just went to sleep like us last night and it's getting up now."

"Oh," I said. "I hope it had a good rest. Big day today for the sun."

"Anyway, it's almost time to meet Mr. Moser to raise the flag at the lighthouse," he continued, already on to the next adventure. "He said to meet him up there to help. I'll get Alli."

Off we went, climbing the trail through the woods, passing a couple of cottages nestled along the path as we made our way to the high point of the island. And so began a week of flag-raising and lowering rituals at the lighthouse. It took some diplomacy to manage whose turn it was to raise and lower the flag halyard each day, but it was ultimately a fine lesson in sharing. In the evenings and on days when the fog rolled in, the children became entranced by the big white lighthouse's great nocturnal beam and its fog-induced moaning sound, as we settled into life on this fifty-acre island with no electricity or running water. With its population of perhaps fifty during summer weekdays, everyone was special, and

Let the Lower Lights Be Burning

no one overlooked. And every act was intentional. Drinking water came from the well, which was in the center of the island. That chore usually came after breakfast, which was pancakes on the rustic wooden deck, the burnt pieces fed to either Hank or Stanley, the two resident seagulls. Then both kids would climb into the two-wheeled wooden pushcart, along with our big yellow water jugs, and off we went, like some characters in a Thomas Hardy novel, headed up the path to the well. We played games along the way, guessing how many strokes on the old iron well pump it would take to fill each container. And again, we shared, taking turns as to who did the pumping first. Sometimes we saw a neighbor along our path and shared island news precious to us in our new world, one that seemed far removed from the volatile events of an emerging Iraq-Kuwait war. The way back to the cabin was a rollicking roll down the path with a load of ten gallons of water and about eighty-five pounds of children. Back at the cabin there was one more chore, and we made our way, with a large dish pan, down to a small tidal pool by the sea. Here we used the Joy soap we knew worked well in saltwater, made lots of suds in the tidal pool—and even threw a few clumps at each other—and washed the dishes from breakfast and the night before. Sometimes Hank or Stanley came by, patiently perched on a rock above us in hopes of another pancake scrap.

Later in the afternoon, after some reading or games on the deck, it was time to head up to the tiny island store in search of the Holy Grail: candy bars. Because Dad was a pushover in this department, Mom usually took the kids on this quest to monitor purchases, while Dad stayed on the porch and settled blissfully into a stack of old *WoodenBoat* magazines. In the late afternoon we took a family trip (usually with one or both kids riding in the cart) around to the other side of the island to meet the ferry. We weren't meeting anyone ourselves, but this trip was, I believe, just to view an event focused on arrivals from the outside world. It gave us perspective. We realized we had no yearning to leave with the ferry; now, as islanders who had lived on the mainland, there was no immediate yearning for the world from which it came.

Faithfully, after dinner, as the sun began to recline, we made our way up to the lighthouse to lower the flag. Oh, there was a little squabbling about whose turn it was, but little Alli really wanted to catch the flag rather than lower it, so all was well. Then we said goodnight to the big white giant and the kids scooted off down the trail for home, knowing Mom and fresh gingerbread awaited. I stayed a while. They knew their way by now, and I was not worried. Instead I enjoyed one of life's most magnificent treats, free to everyone: a radiant sunset. No fog tonight, I thought. The giant will be silent. Only its beam will come, there to lead the way, pouring light across the water, to perhaps guide some hapless soul. For the moment, we were on the other side of that, I realized, ashore by the lighthouse's side and safe for now, in a life not filled with stuff, but filled with each other. We were finding our way as a family, experiencing good lessons, in a world with a lot left to learn.

CHANG HO'S MOST ROMANTIC ADVENTURE

I had to wait until June 5, 2016, for the release of critical information regarding *Chang Ho*'s mystery evening abduction in 1999. I have now obtained that information, which reinforces the phrase that "the truth is stranger than fiction." The names will be changed to protect the innocent (me!).

But first some background: As some of you may know from reading my previous book, *Watching for Mermaids*, a certain son (we'll call him A) and I cruised *Chang Ho*, our Cape Dory 25 sloop, along the coast of Maine for many summers while he was a pre-teen and young teen. He never sailed the boat alone, happy just to hang out in the cabin, sleeping and playing his Game Boy. But he was a smart kid—beating me at chess at age 10—and he must have absorbed *Chang Ho*'s functions and nuances just by being there.

Fast-forward a few years to a bright summer morning in Marblehead in 1999, when A, the certain son, was 15. When I climbed aboard *Chang Ho*, ready to go for a short solo sail, something didn't feel quite right. As all boat owners know, we remember exactly how we put away our vessels. I looked around; lines were coiled the way I coil them, and cushions were stacked under the dodger the way I stack them. I opened the cabin; everything down there looked right. I moved forward; halyards were coiled my way. I shook my head, wondering about the origin of this nagging feeling. I headed forward to raise the mainsail. Then I saw it—there! That was NOT how I tie off the mooring pennants. Someone had been aboard. Or worse, someone had taken my boat off the mooring.

I went for my sail, then rowed ashore, puzzling the whole time. Later that day, when I saw a certain son and his certain friend (B—who had slept over), I asked them point-blank: Did you guys take my boat out last night? A, who is one of those rare people with no ability to lie, just looked at me. "Dad, how did you know that?" he asked. "I put the boat back exactly the way you do."

"Almost," I replied. "You missed one detail when you tied off the mooring. I always put three wraps on the bow cleat. You put two. So what happened last night?"

"We went for a sail."

I looked over at B, who just shrugged at me, bleary-eyed. So that's all the information I got back then, though for 16 years I never stopped trying to pry out more.

Fast-forward to 2016. A is 30, and it's a few months before his June wedding. We're at a pre-party. B is invited, and he's over by the bar. I corner him. "You've got to tell me about what happened with the boat," I said.

"Right after the wedding, Mr. Roper. It must be after the wedding. Then we'll tell you, when we're at the wedding, after it's over."

And that's what happened. And here's the story:

It was back in the days of AOL Instant Messenger, before the boys had cell phones or licenses. "B" was at our house for the sleepover. During the course of the evening the boys got to using our home computer and conversing with two cute girls they knew who were also having a sleepover in a home located across Salem Sound. The girls were probably 10 miles away by land but only two miles as the crow flies. The boys had their titillating invitation, but no means of fulfilling it. No car. Too far to walk. No public transportation. No money for a cab.

At this point, though, A and B related the same versions of the evening, the instigating character is still in dispute. According to B, A said, "We'll take my dad's boat. We'll leave after he and Mom are asleep. They'll never know. According to A, B said, "Come on, let's just take your dad's boat." At any rate, while my wife and I slept blissfully, off they went, running down the hill to the water. They launched our dinghy, rowed out to the boat, raised the sails, and somehow navigated across Salem Sound in the dark, persevering, like the challenged Odysseus, to get to the place where two 15-year-old, modern-day Sirens eagerly awaited them in a distant home somewhere near the water on the far shore.

One problem for our romantic voyagers arose: there is no harbor there. So what to do? Ah! There, as if by magic, drawing them in like the Sirens, was a nice big U.S. Coast Guard steel nun buoy with a ring on the top. We'll tie to that, our heroes thought. They put lots of fenders and life jackets around *Chang Ho* to keep her unscathed, rowed ashore to the nearest beach, pulled up the dinghy, and ventured forth to find the maidens, leaving my precious *Chang Ho* bobbing through the night tied to a federal navigation aid.

Once they were ashore and got their bearings, they determined that they'd miscalculated by about two miles; undaunted, they trudged along in the middle of the night to find the right home. And when they did, to hear it told, the rest of the evening was pure bliss, well worth the quest.

As the sky lightened with the coming of dawn, our gallant adventurers headed back to sea, arriving at my mooring as the sun greeted a new day. Their hearts and minds afloat in blissful thoughts, they put *Chang Ho* back just the way they found her.

Almost.

ELSA'S DANCE CARD

Instead of sailing, this morning I was transported to Fargo, North Dakota, in the Roaring 20s; well, sort of. On the porch today my wife and I uncovered a real treasure: a box of her mother Elsa's dance cards from Fargo High School in the 1920s. Elsa was a lovely lady, so much so that I named my boat after her. Perhaps some of you are old enough to remember dance cards, those cards the young ladies tied to their wrists at dances. They were numbered inside, and a small looped string with a pencil attached went from the card to the hopeful young lady's wrist. If a young man wanted a dance, he gently lifted the lady's scented hand, took the pencil, and put his name on the next open number on her dance card. Elsa must have been quite popular; we found an entire photo album filled with dance cards. And every dance card was full.

Which brings me to the other *Elsa*. She was invited to a rafting party at a yacht club float last week. Well, that's not exactly accurate. I initially asked if she could come. You see, I'm proud of my old sloop. I wanted her to be the belle of the ball, even though I've always known that she would never be the shiniest and certainly never the skinniest girl at the float. But she got invited. We'll make space for her, they said.

At 30 feet, compared to so many others, *Elsa* is not a tall girl. Around her middle, at ten-and-a-half feet, she may be a tad thick, I'll admit. And certainly, at 12,000 pounds, she's off the chart for height/weight ratio. Finally, at 33 years of age, her clock is indeed ticking.

"We're going to a party, *Elsa*," I said to her as I climbed aboard from her little sister, a small rowboat I'd built years ago. She seemed to perk up a bit at that, bouncing on the wake of a passing powerboat. (Well, maybe that's too perky a word; 'slowly lumbering upward' may be the better turn of phrase). "I don't have time to shine you up, old girl," I said out loud as I raised her faded, patched-up, 33-year-old mainsail, "but I'm sure you'll fit in." (So maybe I lied; but it was true that at the time I didn't know who would be coming to the floating dance party.) We sailed out of Salem Harbor and headed for Marblehead. Even with the breeze, our windward performance wasn't great. But that was something we barely noticed anymore. What we had was quality time, not speed. After all, what is quality time but the valued measurement of each passing second? What was important for us now was to go, to mingle, to hold our heads high. No more of those lonesome Maine coves with only the ospreys for company. It was time to blossom.

"We'll put you way down at the end," they said to us as we approached the yacht club float. "There should be enough water there for your boat." And then, there we were, in the door and at the dance, even if it was at the back of the hall. But something wasn't right. Big, beautiful, shiny boats pulled in. One had gleaming stainless steel turnbuckles on her shrouds and varnish work on deck that made *Elsa* and me look down at our keel and feet, respectively. The others pulled in ahead of us, garnering attention as they entered the ball. The biggest, shiniest boat put out two signs boldly declaring: NO SHOES.

"Well, we don't mind shoes," I said aloud. "Maybe you'll meet some people who don't want to take off their shoes, *Elsa*," I said.

Elsa's Dance Card

Two docks away I could just make out a man in a white shirt and black bow tie setting up a bar on the float, complete with hors d'oeuvres. The bar was next to the biggest, shiniest boat. Crowded around the bar and piling onto the shiniest boat (sans shoes) were most of the people at the party. "Well, how about a cocktail?" I said to no one in particular (since there *was* no one in particular), "but we better stay here and drink our own booze in case someone comes down this way and wants to see *you*." No one came. I began thinking about that lonesome Maine cove. I sensed *Elsa* did too, and wanted to leave the party before anyone noticed she'd come.

Then something happened. Someone from up by the shiny boats got bored (or just decided to go for a walk) and headed our way. I thought of that green waterline slime I hadn't removed before the party and figured we'd be passed over. We smiled demurely. "Welcome aboard... ah, if you'd like," I said timidly. He looked *Elsa* over. "Quite a beam on her," he said. Then he looked at her wonderful, commodious cockpit, with the wrap-around stern seat, wooden wheel, and old bronze fittings. "Nice," he said. And by God he came aboard. It was Elsa's first dance. When he went below, we knew we had him. He looked at the five distinctive gimbaled kerosene lamps. He looked at the heavy bronze opening ports and the solid varnished wood everywhere. He looked at the watercolors and pictures on her cabin bulkheads, including the portrait of her namesake. Then he sat down on the canvas-covered bunk, looked around some more, nodded and said, "Now *this* is a boat." Eventually, he left and went back to the other end of the party. "There," I said to Elsa. "You have appeal, even in this crowd. See?"

There was a knock on the hull. It was the same man, and he'd brought back his wife and two friends. "You have to see it inside," I heard him say.

"Welcome aboard... if you like," I said again.

And so, they came. And after they left, others came, saying they had to see her inside. Soon we had eight people in the cabin and others waiting in the cockpit. In hindsight, I'm sure the other boats were even more popular, but at that moment, as the smallest, fattest and oldest boat at the end of the line of floats at the party, we were somebody.

Our dance card was full.

WHY I LOVE RUSSIANS

For my 50th birthday my wife gave me a circumnavigation of Newfoundland on a Russian icebreaker. One might question her intent, sending her husband on a trip around 'The Rock' at midlife. One might even suspect an ulterior motive. But the confounding element was that it appeared that she truly wanted to come along. How lucky can a husband be?

Our dented, extra-thick steel chariot was one *Lyubov Orlova*, named after (ok, you *Jeopardy* fanatics, you have ten seconds): yes, it was after the famous theatre actress, gifted singer, and first recognized star of Soviet cinema.

We boarded her in St. John, Newfoundland. Honestly, at $535 US for the week for everything, including three meals and mid-afternoon snacks, I wasn't expecting much; in fact, a part of me just hoped to make it back. Old 'Lova' (as I grew to affectionately call her) awaited the sixty of us, her expedition tourists, in our polar fleece hats and orange jackets, as we filed down the pier toward the gangway. It took us along a crumpled steel hull that reminded me of a soup can rescued halfway through the kitchen compactor cycle.

"As you know dear, I'm not the worldliest guy in any culinary sense, but I do hope we do not have a Russian chef," I said to my wife as we climbed the rickety metal boarding platform. "And just a quick quote from *The Guardian*'s culinary review that I happened to peruse before we left home: 'At its worst, Russian food is lumps of unidentifiable, grisly meat served with undercooked potatoes.'"

But then I spied Natasha at the top of the gangway. Nothing lumpy, unidentifiable or grisly there. I turned to my wife, who didn't appear to have noticed me notice Natasha, and said quickly, "I'll be cool with the food no matter what, honey, because it's not about the food." She rolled her eyes. "Sweet cabin girls, huh, Dave," was all she said. We'd been together 20 years.

Anyway, off we went, Lova's big, slow-turning engine helping her lumber away and through the majestic high-cliff entrance of St. John Harbour. Things were looking up. There was a Canadian chef (good), a small private cabin for us way down in the bowels of the ship (close to the engine room and warm), a naturalist and historian (very good), and free roam of the entire ship, including the bridge (the best).

And of course, there was Natasha. She was assigned to make up our cabin each morning. My wife befriended her and learned she hadn't seen her family in a year and a half. She had taken this job to try to save some desperately needed money. Standing to the side of the tiny cabin, I tried to look thoughtful, sensitive and cool in my matching fleece outfit.

I'll fast forward the tape to get to the good stuff since, by now, you all figure that this is about Natasha. We steamed along the north coast of Newfoundland to Terra Nova National Park in search of moose, lynx, bald eagles, and carnivorous pitcher plants, proceeded to L'Anse aux Meadows, where Norseman Leif Erikson is thought to have founded Vinland in 1000 AD, continued across the Strait of Belle Isle to Red Bay in Labrador, then continued on to Newfoundland's Gros Morne National Park. There we climbed Precambrian cliffs and searched for giant arctic hare before heading over to the St. Pierre and Miquelon islands for a taste of France and the history of bootlegging. Our final stop was

Why I Love Russians

Francois, a remote fishing outport community; with a population of 124, it was accessible only by boat or helicopter.

Now what's important here is that no vessel the size of Old Lova, and certainly not Old Lova herself, had ever squeezed into this harbor. It looked impossible. Of course, I had to be on the bridge with my Russian 'friends' as we attempted the entrance. The captain, like 100 percent of the entire Russian population, was a chain smoker. It was tense; I didn't need to know Russian to understand that. Fifteen minutes later, we were inside the deep fiord harbor, anchored under 900-foot cliffs. The captain, a gruff-looking, unshaven man in a navy pea coat, glanced at me as he collapsed in his chair. "Dat vuzz a three-cigarette entrance," he said. The tiny town of Francois lay before us, nestled along a boardwalk at the foot of these majestic overhanging rocks.

We boarded our Zodiacs and headed ashore. The townspeople were throwing a party and dance for us. It was a magical and long night. My wife gave up before I did and took one of the Zodiacs back to the ship. I couldn't get enough of the place, and after the party I walked along the waterfront before catching the last boat back. I was the final one of the 60 of us. A full moon rose over the mountains and the Lova's stern as I thanked the first mate and climbed the ship's ladder. The ship was asleep; even most of the deck lights were out. I decided to climb to the afterdeck observation platform to get a good view of the moon before going to my cabin. As I climbed, I heard music. It was a sultry, seductive, belly dance kind of music. And there before me, under the glow of one of the ship's yellow deck light, alone on the spacious steel top deck, was Natasha. The seductive rhythm rose from a boom box by her feet as she danced before me, giving a new level of meaning to the word undulation. I started to back away so as not to spoil her private moment. But then she looked up at me. Embarrassed, I tipped my fleece hat, nodded, and began to back away again. In a serpentine manner, she moved toward me, making a 'come hither' gesture with her right arm.

Later, when I returned to our cabin, my wife was still awake. A small light was on by her bunk bed. "Glad you made it back; I was worried," she said as I gently closed the door. "Remarkable spot," she continued, as she rolled over and turned off the light. The moon shown through our big round porthole, bathing me in a gauzy half-light.

"Magical," I said. "Just magical."

CONVERSATIONS IN THE CABIN

There's always been something special about conversations in the cabin. Maybe it's the feeling of having made harbor, perhaps after a long day at sea, the anchor dug in nicely, the stinging spray and wind now gone from our faces. Somehow, fears and trepidations get extinguished in the calm of the womb-like den as we're now removed, sequestered from the outside world. Somehow, the utter privacy of the cabin, the sense that we're anchored out, not tethered to anyone or anything, grants us permission to really talk, perhaps even let down our guard, free up a few secrets, or finally have the time just to tell some stories to a captive audience.

I've been fortunate to have had many times like this with many lovely people over fifty-plus years of cruising—stories from my wife, son, daughter, father, brothers, and close friends. It's uncanny, but not one ever seemed to hold back in the cabin. It's as if it were a sanctuary.

One night was extra special. I was about 50, my dad about 85, and we were aboard *Elsa*, my 40-year-old sloop, anchored off one of those alluring wooded islands of Merchant's Row in Maine's Penobscot Bay. After a long day's sail and having finished some just-right steak tips from the stern grill, my dad and I had retired to *Elsa*'s cozy cabin. I lit the lamp, poured a couple more glasses of wine, and we settled in.

"Pop, tell me about the Navy and World War II," I asked, knowing I was asking him to reach back over fifty years.

"Ah, my naval career. Well, first, I was no war hero. You need to know that. It all began on an old four-stack destroyer built in the '20s; most of these ships had already been mothballed, but a few were used for NROTC training, and that's why I was on board, a young officer fresh out of Yale. A real greenhorn."

Dad looked amused, then looked down, lost in a memory; I could tell it was a good one.

"I remember the head on board ship, a room on the aft deck, about 15 feet long. A trough for sanitary use ran the length, and a steady stream of sea water came in at the forward end, passed under one, two, three, four, or five squatting rear ends and exited (with its loads) at the after end and overboard. Well, the regular sailors had fun with us NROTC boys. A wise guy at the forward end would light some bunched-up toilet paper and let the stream carry it down under the several innocent bottoms sitting downstream. But this trick could only be done once every NROTC voyage as word spread very quickly."

"Let's flip to the action, Pop. You must have seen some action when the war started. You were in the Pacific, right? Unless maybe you don't want to talk about that."

He smiled. "I was lucky. The closest I got to being on the direct receiving end of the hell of war was an urgent dispatch. You see, my longest duty was in the Pacific, on the USS *Nitro*, an ammunition ship—why the name was plastered on her bow in huge letters I never understood! Kind of like pasting a target to your back. Anyway, I was a young officer and oversaw a deck of sailors including a crew handling the aft deck 3-inch anti-aircraft gun. Then I advanced to communications officer, keeping code books, coding machines, and seeing to the message distribution in the ship and to the Navy outside."

"Must have been some interesting things you were privy to," I said.

"Well, two come to mind. I'll never forget either one. As we were headed into the Panama Canal on December 7, 1941, I received, not coded, but in plain English, this message:

URGENT DISPATCH X AIR RAID ON PEARL HARBOR X THIS IS NOT DRILL

Seems the Navy didn't want an ammunition ship in the Panama Canal in case the Japanese hit that next."

Dad took a sip of his wine, turned and looked aft at the dwindling light in *Elsa*'s companionway, then looked back at me. "And there was a special coded message that was about your oldest brother."

"Really?"

"You see, official messages couldn't be personal in nature, so my friend Curtis, back home, who was also a lieutenant, informed me of something real important with this message:

MSG FOR LIEUTENANT ROPER X SHIPMENT MERCHANDISE ARRIVED X EXCELLENT CONDITION X OUTSIDE THREADS X NET WEIGHT SEVEN AND ONE HALF POUNDS

"Code for a baby boy!"

"Right you are!"

I could see Dad was getting tired. "Okay, just one more question. What about your captains? You must have had some interesting captains."

"Many. One captain during my long tour on the *Nitro* was Captain Clifford Robertson, a portly man with the hobby of model making, which he did aboard ship. Now, in the hot Pacific we were accustomed to wearing any sort of uniform at sea, one being white trousers and an undershirt—even some of the chiefs dressed that way; sometimes even the captain! One hot day Captain Robertson had taken his model down to the crowded carpenter shop and begun using the bandsaw. One of the chiefs arrived to repair a critical item of the ship's gear and needed the same saw. Coming up from behind and being improperly held up by what appeared to him to be just another seaman, he said, 'Shove over, Fatty, some of us have real work to do.' I can only imagine the look on that chief's face when the ship's captain turned around to face him!"

Dad gave a big yawn and smiled. "Anyway, thanks for taking the old man cruising. There's just nothing like it." He stretched out on his bunk, fluffed his pillow, and pulled the blanket up around him. I reached up to turn down the cabin lamp. "Anyway, your old man was no war hero."

I looked over at him and smiled.

"I wouldn't want it any other way," I said.

FRIGHTENING LIGHTNING

When I first flew out to tiny Hector International Airport in Fargo, North Dakota, I was on a new-boyfriend-meets-the-parents mission. When I got off the plane, no one was there to meet me. Well, I'll just step outside and grab a cab, I thought. I pushed open the door, expecting the bustle of an airport ground transportation system; instead I found only the sound of crickets chomping their way through the prairie. My ride finally showed, and off my new girl and I went to meet the parents in their cozy 1920's lake cottage in Detroit Lakes, Minnesota. "Dad has several boats; that should keep you happy," Mary Kay (my wife of 38 years now) told me. The next day Bob, my future father-in-law, proudly showed me his 20-foot D scow sailboat and his stern drive powerboat, both of which sat just out of the water on their boat lifts. They each had full covers over them; underneath, their webbed retaining straps looked like giant seatbelts. "What's with the straps?" I asked Bob gave me a knowing half-smile and looked across the lake to the south. "Storms can get really intense out here," he said.

"Yeah, but these are big boats and it doesn't seem you'd need these straps for..."

"You stay around long enough, and you'll see," he said. "Let's go in for some ice cream and pie."

A couple of years later, a year after his daughter and I were married, I found out what Bob meant about intense. Maybe he should have said weird.

My new wife and I had been sleeping soundly in the cottage's front bedroom, maybe 75 feet from the lake. That night had been unusually still as we drifted off. The old white-and-blue cotton curtains hung limp from their wooden poles above the wide-open windows. About one in the morning we awoke to a rumble and then a crash.

"One's coming," my new wife said, as she shot out of bed and threw on her robe.

"One what?" I asked, rubbing my eyes.

"One from across the lake."

I expected some 400-foot-tall Gila monster from a cheap horror movie to come wading toward us from the other shore.

"Can get bad," she continued. "We need to close all of the windows."

When it hit, we were back in our bedroom, all closed in, sitting on the edge of the bed with the curtains tied back so we could view the storm. It was the blackest night I have ever seen. Then the wind came, wailing like a banshee through the mast and rigging of the D scow on its boatlift, and then crashing against the old windows of the cottage. I thought about Bob's tie-down straps. Even though the lake is less than three miles wide, the waves crashed as if they were falling on an ocean lee shore. Then there was the lightning. Frightening lightning.

"That light's coming at us at 186,000 miles per second; I bet you can't duck in time," I joked.

"Shhhh!" my wife said. "Listen. I hear something."

She was right. It sounded like an old Maine lobster boat: bup bup bup bup.

"What IS that?"

Frightening Lightning

"Sounds like a boat out there. Right off the dock."

"That's impossible. Nobody could be out in the lake now."

And then, as quickly as it started, the wind stopped.

But not the noise. Bup bup bup bup....

"Someone's out there in a boat in this stuff; either that or they're stealing Dad's powerboat."

"That's impossible," I said again, pulling on my shorts. "I've got to go out there and find out." We headed downstairs, past the fireplace, to the front door by the lake.

"Grab something to protect yourself if it's a thief," my dear wife said. "I'll be right behind you." And so—and this is easily one of the most idiotic things I've ever done—I grabbed a fire iron from the fireplace, held it up in the air (think: lightning rod) and marched through the front door.

It was still pitch black, but it was clear that the sound came from the dock. The sailboat was safe on its lift. And so was the powerboat, still fully covered and strapped down. But the powerboat was running! The bup bup bup bup [see previous comment] had been coming from the stern drive, which was exhausting above water [what do you mean, 'exhausting above water'? Maybe it's a nautical term I don't know.] due to the boat being on the lift. Realizing that the engine would overheat soon, I snapped off the cover over the steering wheel and controls to turn it off. But there was no key in the ignition. "I must be dreaming," I said aloud.

"The key is on the hook in the front of the cottage; I'll get it," my wife said. When she returned, I put the key in the ignition, turned it to ON and then back to OFF. The motor stopped. And so does this story. Almost.

For years my father-in-law just rolled his eyes when we related what happened. Everybody did. Even the locals. One summer a couple of years later, my wife said, "Why not ask old Clem? He runs the marina on the other end of the lake. He's seen everything on this lake for 75 years. See if he rolls his eyes." And so, we took the powerboat over to his place. He was bent over, fiddling with an old Coke machine by his docks.

"Quick question for you, Clem," I said. "You ever see lightning start up a boat's engine?" Still kneeling, he reached into his pocket, grabbed two quarters, put them in the machine, banged it once, and a can fell into the catch slot. "Good, that's fixed," he said. Then he got up slowly and looked at me. "Yup," he said. "Seen it happen." He looked across the lake and then at the heavens. "Takes some real frightening lightning though."

So there. Another true story.

You can ask old Clem.

But he's probably dead by now.

Frayed, Frozen and Broken Knots

WHEN THE MOMENT'S RIGHT

If you watched the World Series several years ago you may have seen the television commercial showing that Viagra guy with the $80 haircut 'sailing' a production 30-footer. When the wind starts to blow (approximately 5 knots!) and the mainsheet block's shackle breaks away from the boom, the Viagra guy, as the commercial puts it, 'knows what needs to be done!' He takes a short piece of line and fixes the problem MacGyver-style without breaking a sweat. As he sails off, self-assured, barely moving upwind on a starboard tack, we sailors on our couches at home notice something odd: His jib clew is hauled tight to starboard, the upper leech is to port and the rest of the jib is begging to be let go to port and straining against the mast. In short, he's backwinded. Being backwinded is like trying to ride a horse still tied to the hitching post. No one's going anywhere. Still, the Viagra guy pretends to sail on serenely and makes no move to release the jib sheet. Perhaps the blood has gone from his head to another extremity. Or perhaps it's just that Madison Avenue doesn't care.

Maybe the Viagra guy's a slow learner. I know I am. A few years ago, in a magazine article, I divulged to readers that my first wife once poured a quart of semi-gloss topside paint over my head. It was a hot, humid August day in the boatyard, and our neglected wooden sloop was still not launched. Everyone else was out sailing. I made some disparaging remark about the way my then-wife was painting. It was totally uncalled for. She poured the paint on my head and walked away. I would have done the same thing.

Fast forward 35 years. Dave's still learning but doing better after 30 years of marriage to his true love. It's early September, and Mary Kay and I are on *Elsa*, headed to one of the islands in Salem Sound to do some final edits on the galleys of a book I had finished that summer. Mary Kay is a brilliant editor, and I was looking forward to discussing more of her comments and adjustments to the manuscript. I was also looking for a mooring pennant hanging from the mooring ball close off Misery Island's rocky shore. But there was no pennant, only a shackle at the top of the mooring ball. "What may I do to help?" Mary Kay asked, as she always does. "I've got it fine, thanks," I said, as I always say. (You see, Roper, like that Viagra guy, has to do it himself; he 'knows what needs to be done.')

As we approached under power, I aligned *Elsa* with the mooring, put the engine in neutral, grabbed a short piece of line, ran forward, and lay on the starboard deck, ready to reach down and feed the line through the shackle. Mary Kay moved to the wheel. My approach had been good. However, my feed through the mooring shackle was not. I missed, and we began to slide by, headed toward the rocky shore. I leaned farther over the rail, grabbing the shackle, trying to stop *Elsa*'s six tons of forward motion. I almost went overboard. "Reverse! Reverse!" I shouted. "Put her in reverse!" I looked over my shoulder at my wife. There was an uncertain look on her face as she stared at the two levers by the wheel. "Is it the big one or the little one?" she asked anxiously. "The big one! The big one!" I yelled as my arm stretched in a Gumby-like manner. "But reverse is forward. Remember? Forward is reverse."

Fifteen minutes later, once safely moored, all was silent on board. I was angry. She felt bad. Intuitively, each of us knew how the other felt. The moment wasn't right; saying anything more would have only aggravated the situation. So, I did something it took me six decades to learn: I shut up, went down below, sat down, gave myself a time out, and thought about the situation rather than speaking. What I thought about, though, was our dishwasher. Why, after all these years, couldn't I load our dishwasher properly? Because I didn't pay attention. Because I didn't do it enough. Because I didn't know the consequences of loading dishes incorrectly. So, what was the difference between that and this recent scene? Nothing. Why should Mary Kay remember which lever is which when I'm almost always at the wheel? How could she know which lever is which when neither the clutch nor the throttle lever is marked? And then my yelling "Reverse is forward!" amidst it all? What's that all about? (Well, it's that way because when I put in a rebuilt transmission a few years ago I messed up a bit regarding the linkage. Ever since, if you want to go forward, you put the engine in reverse... kind of a counter-intuitive thing to remember, I admit.)

But this time, after my time out in the cabin, the moment became right. My blood, for once, had been in my brain. I had shut up. And it had become a happy and productive afternoon. Lasting much longer than four hours.

AFTER TOUCHING LEAVES OF THREE, DON'T GO OUT TO SEA

I was run over by a Boston Whaler. I heard over a Bermuda AM radio station that I was assumed lost at sea. I put 314 passengers through a Mississippi River tornado. I've been downstream from a busted sewage-holding tank. And those are just for starters. But nothing has compared to my encounter with the dreaded *Toxicodendron radicans* and its internal alien monster, urushiol.

It all started innocently enough. It was July, and time for me to head to Maine, as I have done for the past 30 years. I usually go solo (it allows me to sing loudly and off-key for three days); my wife, Mary Kay, drives up to meet me. Before I left this time, she asked me if I might clear the weeds and rampant vines from our back hill. "But cover yourself VERY well," she said. "There's a rumor of poison ivy lurking on that hillside."

"I don't get poison ivy," I said confidently.

She gave me that 'do what I say' look. "Just because you've never gotten it doesn't mean you won't get it."

"What's the big deal anyway? Isn't poison ivy something little camper kids get; the ones you see covered in pink from that calamine lotion."

Anyway, the day before I was to head offshore, I cleared the hillside.

The next day, about twelve miles off Cape Ann and headed east, I felt a silly, nagging little itch on my left wrist. Whatever. I was making good time toward the Isle of Shoals, where I planned to stop for the night. I knew I would arrive just before the thick black dungeon cloud and thunderstorm that, I swear, hits me every year at about 6:45, just after I pick up a mooring there.

So, what's with this itching? Now it's on my other wrist. Heck, now it's going up my right arm. Better wash it off. Mary Kay said something about this urushiol oil not being too good on human body parts. What about calamine lotion? None of that aboard. And that's for sissy camper kids. Pinot grigio? Ah, plenty of that behind the port bunk. That might do the trick; at the very least it will stop the itching. (The trick, by the way, is to pour it down your throat and not over the poisoned body parts; it works extremely well that way, when taken in some quantity, until about 0200 hours, when it has worn off and you awake itching and scratching yourself like a maniac.)

Two days later, by the time I reached the eastern part of Casco Bay and my wife came aboard, I had wrapped myself in gauze. Mary Kay fears little in life, but poison ivy terrifies her. "Did you sit on my bunk? Did you touch this? What towels did you use? You need to stay on your side of the boat from now on. Do you have Calamine lotion?"

"No, but I have something better. It could even work around the clock if I took it non-stop, but I don't think that's the best idea if I'm captain."

"What are you talking about?"

"It's called pinot grigio. No prescription. You just need a proper ID. Yes, it's more expensive than Calamine but, heck, it's all I have to treat this dreaded thing." She rolled her eyes. "Might even be an antidote for you, dear. I'll share some with you. In your very own glass, of course."

After Touching Leaves of Three, Don't Go Out to Sea

Things got worse. It started to rain. For three days. And the pinot grigio was running low. One night, at about 2:01, I awoke in such as state that I considered jumping into the icy Maine water. My hope was not to eradicate the itching—I now believed it would never go away—but to drown. "Why don't you just leave the boat here and go home?" Mary Kay said from her side of the cabin.

"Why, so I can itch at home?" I replied. "If I'm going to itch, I'm going to do it on my beloved boat on my beloved Maine coast with my beloved wife."

When I dropped Mary Kay off in Brunswick, we were able to take her car and find a CVS store. I hurried in and headed for the pharmacy section. "Excuse me, but where is your Calamine lotion?"

"What type do you need, sir—Calamine or Caladryl? I mean, how bad is the condition?" the pharmacist asked.

At this point, showing him any body part would do, but I held up my left inner wrist, a particularly gruesome manifestation of the dreaded *Toxicodendron radicans*.

"Oh," he said with a withering look, "that'd be Calamine; but you're close to a staph infection."

I bought the Brunswick CVS's entire stock of Calamine lotion, along with enough gauze to re-supply Mass General's emergency room. My wife dropped me off back at the boat. I went below, took off my clothes, and had myself a Calamine shower. Then I headed to sea.

I now had Calamine and pinot grigio. And good, warm weather. But it just got worse. My clothes aggravated the poison ivy. So, on the last day, I took them off. All of them. This was fine offshore. Quite nice, and I really got used to it. As I rounded Cape Ann and adjusted my course close to the Eastern Point breakwater in Gloucester, I began to encounter other boaters and sailed close by a young family anchored and fishing from their little cabin cruiser. Forgetting that the entirety of my sartorial splendor consisted of only a large straw hat and sunglasses, I raised my gauze-wrapped arms and waved. No one waved back. We all know why.

A FROZEN MARRIAGE

Along about 1975, in the fifth year of my first marriage, I bought a pair of hiking boots. I'd never had a pair of hiking boots before. I'd never been a real hiker. Never put a pack on my back and gone. Anyway, they were sitting in the window of this small Minneapolis shoe store. Actually, they were standing there; this fine a pair of boots could never sit.

"Look at those boots," my wife said. "They're just what you need."

"They are?"

"Of course. You've never had a really good pair of boots."

We went in. The door jingled. A cute little shoe salesman with round glasses and a bald spot on the top of his head came over right away. He looked glad to see somebody. We were the only ones in the store and, judging from the bland storefront with the faded "SHOES—PAY LESS" sign, we probably had been the only ones in a long time.

"Help you folks?" he asked, smiling, leaning his upper torso toward us, his hands behind his back, his legs straight and together, as if he were a servant in an old English manor house. I was worried he wouldn't be able to straighten up.

"Those boots," my wife said, pointing. She always ran the show in places like this, and rightly so, for I was never any good at it, would never get right to the point. My turn came later, when it came to trying them on, though even then my wife would tell me whether they fit or not.

"Can you move your toes? You always buy shoes that are too small, and your toes end up freezing." She was right, of course. I always did buy hurriedly, not wanting to seem like an indecisive, nitpicking sap of a person. "These are great," I'd say, my toes bent over double inside the shoe. I'd just want to get out of there.

This time I wasn't going to get away with it. "We're taking our time, and you're going to be comfortable in these," my knowing wife said. The salesman was holding up the boots in the window. He was still leaning forward in that peculiar stance of his. I wondered if he had a birth defect or something.

"You're looking at the best hiking boot made," he said, leaning and addressing my wife. No one paid much attention to me at this point. But I knew my turn was coming. Only I could try them on, though the thought didn't particularly excite me. The salesman handed one of the boots to my wife. She studied it. I squinted, trying to see the price tag. I thought I saw a 6.

The salesman went into his pitch while she examined the boot. "The leather is the very finest cowhide and layered for protection and insulation. They'll be cool in the summer and warm in the winter. The sole is the very best—Vibram—and it will take ages to wear it out. And the extra layer between it and the inside of the boot will dispel any conducted heat or cold from the synthetic Vibram soles. You get the best of both worlds."

I stepped closer to the boot, vaguely interested now. My wife had the thing practically inside out, examining the dark recesses of its sole. I looked at the salesman. He wasn't nervous; he was confident, like it really was a good boot. "Hmmm," I said, leaning forward, pretending to look at the stitching along the insole. There was a 6 in the price tag, and it was followed by an o, and then a period.

"Hiking boots," I said quickly, shaking my head. "I don't do any hiking."

My wife had finished her examination. "Don't let the price bother you," she said, not looking at me but at an overall view of the boot.

"What about the price?" I asked, pretending I had no idea. She smirked at me. We'd been five years together.

"Forget the price," she said, convinced now of the boots' merit. "These boots will be good for you. They'll do things well." The salesman was smiling, nodding, still leaning. "We'll start by trying on a size 9," my wife said, more to the boot than to either of us.

Why don't we start with a size 5, and you go hiking, I thought, looking over at my wife. But deep down I knew it was I who needed the boots. It was just that I hated this, hated shoe stores, hated diddling around with shoe salesmen. I knew a grueling process lay ahead. We started with a size 9.

"Perfect," I said, reaching down to unlace the boot. My wife reached down to my toes.

"We'll try a 9½," she said.

"More perfect," I said. "This is it." (Now that I think back on it, there was room for two more sets of toes to leisurely wander around inside those 9½s.)

"Let's just try an 8½ to see," my wife said. The salesman went for an 8½. "I want you to really be sure, "she told me, patting my knee and sensing my agony. "You always rush into things, and that often gets you in trouble."

"Good enough," I said about the 8½, looking toward the street—and freedom. My toes were cramped into the shoe like so many college students in a phone booth.

"The 8½ runs a little small," the salesman said, looking at my contorted face. I had to agree.

"The 9 is perfect," I said with complete assurance. My wife looked at me quizzically, her head tilted. "Really," I said. "Really, the 9 is perfect. We went back to the 9, and I walked out, sole owner of those boots.

They began to become a part of me. They probably were the best hiking boot money could buy, though I never wore them for hiking. I wore them for everything else, though. They began to mold themselves around the curves and arches and odd protrusions of my feet. They kept my feet warm in the winter, and they never leaked, though it is true that almost weekly I slavered them with mink oil, shoe polish, and silicone. They made me taller, which made me feel more significant, which was something I needed.

In winter the waffled Vibram soles never slipped, never let me down. I walked with a steady, self-assured gait. Though my mother-in-law and a few others greeted them with apprehension (the waffled soles were adept at bringing the outdoors inside people's houses), I loved them. Sixty dollars, it seemed, was a small price to pay for the new me.

The seasons changed, summer came, and my older brother arrived on his new motorcycle. He pulled up in front of the house, the engine of the bike idling quietly, smoothly, perfectly. "It's the finest motorcycle money can buy," he said proudly. "Even the grease rag that comes with it is monogrammed with the name of the bike."

"Wow," I said, "it's beautiful." It really was. It was summer, and I had on my sneakers, but I thought of my boots, oiled up nice and tucked away in my closet. I looked at my brother. He was so proud, so satisfied. He patted the gas tank.

"Hand painted," he said. The motor idled on, flawlessly. "You're lucky," I said. "I could never afford that."

"Well, it wasn't cheap, but it's the Rolls Royce of motorcycles. Should last as long as I do."

"Yeah," I said. "Just like my boots."

"Your what?"

"My boots. My hiking boots. I showed them to you, remember?"

He smiled. "Oh, those," he said, "why don't you go put them on and we'll race." He had that sarcastic look of his that I never liked. Then he started to laugh. "Give me a call when you get them tuned up, and we'll do a standing quarter-mile together."

Then he roared off. Flawlessly. He could be a real jerk.

I tried to tell lots of people about my boots that first year. I tried to tell them how they made me feel, how warm they were, and how perfectly suited I thought we were for each other. But hiking boots just didn't measure up, conversationally, with things like motorcycles, or cars, or even cameras. I gave up talking about my boots at parties, gave up telling folks about the Vibram soles or the special layer of insulation; people's eyes just glazed over, or they changed the subject on me in mid-sentence, or moved on to another person, where the talk might go to BMWs or Nikons.

The seasons changed some more. The year changed. The following spring, I bought a motorcycle. It wasn't much, not like my brother's, but it was cheap and tuned up, ready to go. I needed to get away for a while, and the motorcycle seemed like the best way to do it. I put on my hiking boots, tied my pack to the back of the bike, and said goodbye to my wife. It was a different goodbye than we'd ever had before; there wasn't the same sense of sadness, I thought. I listened for the sniffling as I hugged her. It wasn't there. I got on the bike and headed down the Mississippi River Road to New Orleans, twelve hundred miles away.

One hundred miles from Hannibal, Missouri, it started to get hot, and I got really tired. The boots, true to the salesman's word, kept my feet cool, but my sitting position on the bike made my rear end extremely sore. I changed position, moving my feet to the back foot pegs of the bike. It redistributed the weight and helped immensely. It also put my right boot against the exhaust pipe and burned the leather, leaving the once-smooth cowhide black and indented. It ruined the day. I stopped in Hannibal at a campground for the night. It was a short distance to town. I jogged in, both to loosen my stiff muscles and to see the Mark Twain museum before it closed. I loosened my muscles anyway.

The next day the bike got me to Memphis, though no one seemed to care. People at gas stations and road rests went about their business around me. It wasn't like in the movies. No one came over, looked at my pack and bedroll and, green with envy, said, "Hey, man, wow, where you headed? Wish I could come along."

I never got the chance to say the "well, hang in there" that I'd practiced. Never got to zoom off in front of them and head into the setting sun. One time I even tried to elicit an envious response. At a Shell station in Portageville, Missouri, I thought I saw a flicker of interest in the eyes of the kid who was pumping gas into my tank. He seemed to glance at my pack and sleeping bag.

"Well-l-l," I said, stretching. "It's been one long, hot ride."

"Yup, hot out," he said.

"Yeah, wel-l-l-l-l, I gotta keep goin'; lot of miles to cover yet."

"Uh-huh. Buck and a half."

"Huh?"

"Buck and a half for the gas, mister."

I paid the kid. He didn't even stay there to watch me start the bike. Bronson and the Lone Ranger are dead.

The third day I made it to New Orleans. It was just as well. Another day would have shaken the fillings from my teeth. I stayed a week, got drunk on Bourbon on Bourbon Street, fooled around with a girl I met in a bar there, saw Preservation Hall, and left. The ride back to Minnesota was no thrill, believe me.

When I returned there was no marching band. But my wife was there on the porch. She didn't seem particularly glad to see

A Frozen Marriage

me. I showed her my boot. She gave her condolences. I told her about New Orleans, skipping the part about the girl. She listened, distantly.

Three years went by. During those years, I sold the motorcycle, had a brief affair, went through several jobs, and wrote a couple of books, both unpublished. Then last year happened. And now I'm here in this cabin, alone. I came up here to think and write and maybe try again to heal. My old hiking boots are still with me; in fact, they're in front of me right now, on the ledge by the picture window that looks out on a slowly freezing Lake Superior. They are standing there quietly, looking back at me. (Maybe I should turn them around to face the lake.) I'm here at the typewriter. My Great American Novel still isn't going too well. I feel compelled to type something.

From this angle I can't quite see the blackened scar on the right boot, but I know it's there. I should put some brown shoe polish on it. The toe of the left boot is dented in. All the shifting on the motorcycle did that. The laces are frayed but have not yet broken. The inward edges of the Vibram soles are worn down quite a bit, and it causes the boots to lean together. It looks funny from here, like they're holding each other up. The leather is wet from early this morning when I went out for firewood. It's probably only a surface dampness. Still, I don't silicone them as much as I should, or as much as I used to.

Yesterday, to get away from the novel, I did some hiking. I put on my heavy Norwegian wool socks, some woolen long underwear, my blue wool trousers, a wool lumberjack shirt, and my thick wool sweater. I itched something frightful and couldn't sit still. Wool is good incentive for hiking. I went to the window ledge and got my hiking boots. My feet slid into them with the kind of effortless movement that comes from years of molding, the way a pair of hands fold together, the knuckles of the fingers of each hand locking into each other with a smooth, simple grace. It was always harder to get the boots off. Many times I never bothered, and ended up clumping around the cabin with them on, leaving a trail of mud and half frozen pieces of snow behind. Sometimes I'd fall asleep on the couch with them on, only to awaken in the middle of the night to remove them, sleepily, and stumble into the bedroom, soaking my socks in the little puddles of melted snow along the way.

 I laced the boots up tight, put a couple of oranges, some cheddar cheese, my sunglasses, a compass, and a windbreaker into my day pack, grabbed my walking stick, and clumped out the door. I was off on a real hike at last.

 I got far. It surprised me. I am not a physical specimen. My wife told me that my arms are getting flabby and that should do push-ups. A push-up is a highly unpleasant, even tortuous thing; worse, I will venture to say, than the chin-up. If, as humans, we hadn't evolved past the stage of hanging from trees, I would say the push-up had its place, and flabby harms did not. However, today one can exist just fine with flabby arms and, though I would rather not have flabby arms, I would more rather not do push-ups.

 Still, I got far. My legs are rather good. And of course I had the hiking boots. Mostly I was in sight of the lake, walking high on a bluff. There was less than a foot of snow on the ground, and the top inch was fresh from the night before. I picked up a deer trail and began to follow it as it wound its way through a grove of birch. It gave me direction, and I figured, who knows, I might even bump into the deer. The lake was still and quiet, perhaps a hundred feet below my path. It was getting ready to freeze, and lay still under an eerie low fog, a great body settling down to a long winter's sleep.

 I hadn't been up around this part of the lake in a long time, and never in January. It was odd to see it so calm, so lacking in fury. So odd to see winter putting to sleep the largest and most treacherous body of fresh water in the world, a body that could easily snap great ore ships in two.

I walked over to the edge of the cliff. Carefully. It was hard to tell where the edge was. The snow could be deceiving, giving a false sense to the limits of the edge, suddenly making a cliff diver out of the most unlikely of persons, in the most unlikely of seasons. I poked my walking stick into the snow ahead, and worked my way out to the edge. There was a small sapling there, and I grabbed it while looking down. It wasn't big enough to save a squirrel, but at least it was something to hang on to. And if I fell, I wouldn't go alone. They'd find me, weeks later, wedged between a couple big rocks at the bottom of the cliff, my hand frozen around a tiny sapling, its exposed, pencil-sized roots hanging over me in witness to my foolishness. "I guess we can rule out suicide, chief," the Cook County deputy would say. "And common sense," the chief would add, extricating the uprooted twig from my hand. Then he would pause, looking down and noticing something. "Nice boots, though," he'd say, slowly shaking his head.

I decided to move back, and return to the business of following the deer trail. I could see up ahead that the bluffs would decrease in height. I could view the lake there, from a lower level.

It was so quiet. A crow flew overhead, and I was startled by the fact that I could hear the flapping of its wings. They made a whooshing sound, the great black wings displacing the thin winter air. The sound made flying seem more of an effort, and I thought, maybe it's a lot of work being a bird, all that flapping to try to stay up there. Maybe there's not the romance that we think there is.

It all made me think about my novel. The night before I'd made the mistake of reading it over, reviewing the thing right up to where I'd left off that afternoon. Something big was missing, a whole spark; there was nothing to ignite what was there. It was as if I had invented and built an engine, supplied it with combustible fuel, and then become hopelessly perplexed about a way to ignite it. I could not envision a spark plug. I seemed incapable of it. The motor was useless.

My toes were getting that way, too. I'd stood still too long. They felt damp. I moved ahead, following the deer trail as it wound its way down from the bluff to the lake. At the base of the bluff was a half-moon-shaped beach, split in the middle by a river. The deer trail led down to the beach, and I followed. Here and there were packed down spots in the snow. The deer apparently came here at night to rest. I wondered if they thought it safe here, in this place. It did seem secure, tucked in below the high bluffs. I stood there, watching my breath as I exhaled into the now much colder air. The wind had risen and changed course, coming ashore at me from across the great lake.

My toes were so cold they hurt. I moved ahead, deciding to hike inland along the edge of the river. I wiggled my toes, trying to get the circulation going. I'd known that feeling—knew it too well from one day in the woods the year before—and tried to push that thought aside. Maybe today the boots had gotten damp somehow, on the inside. It was obvious that there wasn't enough silicone on them; the snow was staying with the boots, and not being repelled. Well, I'd follow the river in, figuring it would have to cross with the main road after a while, and I'd take that back to the cabin. It wouldn't be as pleasant, taking the road, but it would be quicker and easier, and my toes, which were starting to get numb, would thaw out that much sooner.

The river still flowed under the ice. I could hear it. It rushed along, gurgling with vitality, only to flow into the lake and be smothered by the sound of the now-building waves. I trudged on, trying to weigh my temptation to hurry my pace in the race against the dwindling daylight with the fear of what could come from breaking a sweat; it could mean losing precious body heat and slipping into the strange stages of hypothermia where one loses rational thought, suddenly feels warm, and then begins acting strangely in the face of death. I tried to push that thought away, but it was too vivid, still too timely, and my mind shot me back to that sub-zero day deep in the Minnesota woods a year ago. I visualized her again. She lay there, flat on her back on that bleak, frozen, and isolated white lake. I saw the dense woods on the shore begin to fade as the white-out continued, the rising winds buffeting us, picking up and swirling the snow, seemingly trapping us in the middle of that frozen lake.

~∞~

The year it happened we'd rented a cabin on the property of a remote ski lodge. Even for Minnesota folks, it was too cold for downhill skiing, so we'd headed to the cross-country ski shack on the property and picked up a trail map. The young man in the hut was proud of the new trails he'd cut that prior summer and handed us his new sketch map of the trail loop, which ultimately crossed a small, round lake, and then led back to the lodge. Two, maybe two-and-one-half hours was all it would take, the young man said. My wife looked at the sky and then her watch. "Two-and-a-half hours," she said. "Kind of a late start for this." I fiddled with my skies, eager to go. She looked at the young man. "You're sure about that time frame?" He gave her a half nod. "Yeah, 'bout that I'd say."

"Let's go," I said, and headed into the woods. It was one p.m. There was only one set of tracks on the densely wooded trail, which was well marked every hundred yards with red ribbons tied to branches. The lake, according to our map, was about three quarters of the way along the loop, then the trail crossed the lake and entered the woods again at the far end. We skied on at a steady pace in the now windy and increasingly colder air. Two hours went by. No lake. We moved on. I kept stopping to study the sketch map. More time passed. It seemed to be taking way too long to get to the lake; now it was 3:30. We had to be almost there; it looked from the map to be less than an hour from the lake back to the lodge. Turning around would take us two-and-one-half hours; darkness would overcome us. I knew there would be no help from the moon, given the overcast sky, and we wouldn't be able to see the faint tracks of the trail or the trail markers. So we just kept moving toward the lake. My wife began to slow. I urged her on. She stopped. Just stared. I urged her on. The trail ribbons had now disappeared. All we had in the dwindling light was the gradually eroding set of tracks from that prior skier. We followed them religiously. To my wife behind me I made statements I wasn't sure I believed. "We're almost there, honey. The way the trees are fanning out, the lake must be just ahead."

And finally, it did come. The tracks brought us to the edge of the lake. I could just make out their route across, leading, no doubt, to the trail in the woods on the other side, and then a short length home to a warm cabin. I looked back at my wife in relief, expecting her to pick up the pace now that we'd found the lake. But she lingered—stood still, leaning against a big pine, staring at the trees. I got her moving again, continuing to follow the now barely discernible tracks in the snow. When we reached the middle of the lake, away from the tall pines, the wind got brutal. It swirled around us, kicking up the light snow on the ice. It made the tracks ahead dwindle, then disappear. There was nothing left but the shifting, wind-roiled white surface of the lake stretching into an empty, opaque horizon.

I looked behind me. My wife was on her back, stretched out; her skis, still attached, were splayed at an acute angle to each side of her body. She had unzipped her down parka and removed her wool ski hat. Her eyebrows were frosted; the snot from her nose was frozen halfway down her cheek. A faint smile was on her face.

She looked up at me. "I'm just going to take a little nap now," she said. A strong gust buffeted us, sending her wool hat skittering across the ice until it disappeared in the blowing snow. "NO! NO! NO!" I screamed, leaning down and grabbing her by the front of her jacket. She just lay there, smiling. I could feel the toxic flow of panic climbing up through my body until it erupted as a primal scream; this was absorbed, with seeming indifference, into the wind and snow and trees of the woods around us.

―∞―

A year has gone by since it happened. I haven't cross-country skied since. I was surprised I was even back in the woods again so soon, especially alone. I looked down at my hiking boots, then at the river again, then up at the building waves of Lake Superior.

My toes were now numb and there was no more pain. They were as cold as they could possibly get, though I wasn't worried. I was sure I could walk in my boots without any feeling in my toes. For a while anyway, I knew it would be just the numbness and I'd be okay, clumping along the frozen side of the river, up to the road, and along it to the warm cabin, where my toes would begin to thaw and the pain would start all over again. In a way, though, it would be a welcome pain, a pain meaning that my toes were coming back to life, that they were getting a second chance, a pain that should remind me I ought to silicone those hiking boots more often. Once more, I thought, I've been lucky, just as I was that dying day last year—that day when a young man heard my scream while out on his end-of-day trail check. His first thought was that it was just the screech of the wind; shivering, he'd continued down the trail. Until he remembered the two of us, his sketch map and our late start, and decided to turn back and venture out onto the lake. Where he found us. Just in time.

WHEN ZEUS IS MAD

As we rounded Appledore Island at the Isle of Shoals Saturday afternoon, I crossed my fingers. It was high season, a weekend, and unbelievably hot ashore, so I feared all the moorings in the Shoals' Gosport Harbor would be taken. But it was worse than that: many boats had to raft together, four and five abreast, despite the harbor's complete exposure to the west.

"We may have to anchor," my pal Spencer said.

"That's tough. It's all kelp and ledge," I replied. Then, way down at the head of the harbor, one hundred feet off the stone breakwater, we spied an empty white mooring ball.

"It says PRIVATE," Spencer told me as I rounded *Elsa* up by the pennant.

"Grab it for now," I said.

And so we did, then went below to escape the intense heat and sun.

"Tell me a story about this place," Spencer said, looking out one porthole at the old hotel on Star Island and then out another porthole at Smuttynose Island to the north. So I told him about a chapter in my book, *Watching for Mermaids*, called "Faith, Fear and Fate," about how fate ruled the day on March 6, 1873, when two young women were murdered on Smuttynose Island, all because a train coming into Portsmouth was a day late. "Just a seemingly little thing, a train being late, allowed for a chain of events that led to murder," I said, shaking my head after finishing the story. "Fate's funny."

"Or not so funny," Spencer added.

A few minutes later, feeling sure we'd get kicked off the mooring soon, I said, "Maybe we should just try to set my big anchor, try to get some good holding ground while we still have the energy."

Just then came a knock on *Elsa*'s hull. "See," I said as I popped up, "we're getting thrown off already." But it was Mike, a friend from way back when I led a *Points East Magazine* flotilla, coming over in his inflatable dinghy to say hello. We traded sea stories, and just as he was leaving, I said, "Too bad there aren't any moorings left, Mike. This one's private."

"Oh, you're fine," he replied, looking at the mooring ball. "You're on my friend's mooring. He won't be coming back tonight, and that's a good strong one."

It was that last-minute short comment of mine about moorings that probably saved *Elsa* (and maybe us!) that evening, allowing us to stay put and not try to anchor. No anchor would have held in what was to come.

Fate was on our side—this time, anyway—when it did come an hour later. It came as a wind that I never imagined possible. It came as a ghoulish howling wind that gusted to over 70 miles per hour and came up from the west in under five seconds, turning into a screeching banshee that first emanated from a very strange tubular cloud within a cloud; it came as a wind so strong it laid my six-ton sailboat on her side while it attacked a fleet of perhaps 30 boats, grabbing a handful of them, heavy chain moorings and all, and sweeping them down the quarter-mile open-to-the-west-facing harbor like some crazed Zeus hurtling down a mighty sneeze. Amidst it all, the air turned a strange brown color and the wind sounded like a cross between an ambulance and a freight train. I couldn't see forward, able only to look astern at the giant boulders and the now crashing five-foot seas licking their chops at us. Sometimes I got a partial sight to my port and starboard despite the intense rain and hail. Then, to port, came a two-boat raft of cabin cruisers, still tied together, the broken mooring gear hanging limply off the bow of one of them. They blew by, headed for the seawall behind me, their passengers helpless in the cabin. But instead, they crashed into my friend Mike's 36-foot sailboat, and the three bashed together amidst the maelstrom. Next came a tremendous bang, bang, bang, whack, whack, whack, like machine gun fire. A 45-foot sloop's roller-furling mainsail had rolled itself out in the hurricane-strength winds. I watched it thrash itself to death. Then came a sight that will never leave my memory: As I squinted through the forward-facing dodger window, trying to look upwind, I could just make out a huge looming shape coming at us; it was the blue-striped hull of a 44-foot sailboat, its big white mooring ball and chain dragging impotently off the bow as the vessel came at us at eight knots. Somehow, the captain steered clear and rounded up just ahead of the breakwater.

Then the storm stopped.

I drank a half bottle of wine, bailed my dinghy, and rowed around and took some pictures. One was of a large yacht's captain's chair, perched high up on the rocks minus its captain.

But Zeus claimed no one that evening. All were safe.

Perhaps that was fate as well.

A LOVE STORY AND A GHOST STORY

For three years, Barry was my crew chief aboard a 135′ Mississippi sternwheeler I used to captain on the Upper Mississippi. But he was more than that. He was an incorrigible practical joker and a daredevil. He rode his 1000cc motorcycle at insane speeds, pulling the occasional wheelie. He made up outlandish stories about our stretch of the river and fed them almost daily to our 300 enthralled tourists. Did they know that the Sasquatch was once seen in those woods by Monkey Rudder Bend? And that Mark Twain himself had lived in a cabin near Fort Snelling? And that those large electrical wires strung across the river near the airport—the ones that had those huge orange balls strung through them so planes could see them—well, did they know they were filled with helium to help keep the wires up? It went on and on.

Happy-go-lucky Barry, with his delightful, infectious laugh. He just had fun with people.

He had also fallen in love with a charming young crewmember named Lisa. He smiled even more often. Finally, Barry realized his dream of buying *Dave's Ark*, my houseboat, as I was planning a move back East to the ocean. We consummated the sale, though he told me to keep the deal secret; his parents probably wouldn't approve. All in all, things were going well for this young man.

But life can be fleeting. On a hot summer day that year, between cruises, I had to drive my car to Minneapolis for some supplies. Barry was left in charge of the crew washing down the ship. I returned a couple hours later to find the wharf filled with police cars, fire engines and an ambulance. Terrified, I shot down the stairs and across the gangway. One of my crew, a young man of perhaps 21, stared at me, a shattered, distraught look in his eyes.

"Barry slipped, Cap. From the third deck. Tried to dive off. Slipped. Tried to push away on the way down. I was right there. Hit his head on the main deck guardrail. Disappeared into the river. God, they just found him." He started sobbing.

And so came the mourning. The funeral. I gave the eulogy, looking at Barry's girlfriend, Lisa, and his parents in the front row. And slowly, the healing began. Barry was often in our heads, all of us in the crew. And now he owned my houseboat. After the reception, I told his parents about his secret, and said that I would give them his money back. "We want to keep it, rename it the Barry D in his honor," they said.

"That may not be practical; maybe that's just an emotional response right now," I said.

"No," they replied, "we're going to name it after him."

A tribute. And that's what happened.

The season wound down. There were only a few charters left. I began to pack up the things from my houseboat. That night there was a wedding reception on board the sternwheeler. It was a late one, and passengers finally finished disembarking well after midnight. From the pilothouse, I put on the music the crew liked while they cleaned up and turned up the master amplifier to the standard level of #2 (though Barry had always wanted it LOUD). I locked the pilothouse as required and headed down to the main deck bar to grab a beer.

On the main deck, I watched Barry's girl, Lisa, restocking the bottles at the bar, occasionally stopping to wipe tears away from her eyes. The other crew were busy vacuuming the carpet in front of the bar and around the tables, seeming to move with the music piped in over the 20 overhead speakers. And that's when it happened. The volume shot up five times its level. Everyone stopped. The vacuums stopped. Lisa looked up at me, as did the other crew members.

"Who's been in the pilothouse?" Sean, the new crew chief asked.

"No one," I replied. "It's locked."

The music was blaring.

I shot up the port-side stairs of the first and second decks, unlocked the pilothouse and, not bothering to turn on the light, grabbed the flashlight on the console and shined it up at the master amplifier. It was pegged at #10. I grabbed the knob and turned it back down to 2. Now, I've never SEEN a ghost, but right then, as sure as I'm writing this, I FELT one. Barry's infectious laugh invaded my whole being, my body tingling from head to toe. I shot down three flights of stairs to the live world of the main deck. All the crew were staring at me. "Who turned it up?" Sean asked.

"Barry," I said. They all looked at me. Strangely.

All except Lisa. Who just smiled.

And I knew she'd felt him too.

BEYOND BIG RED—TODDY'S STORY

January 9, 2015: Grouchy's Marina, aboard Cirrhosis of the River

In the dwindling daylight, Wihopa Webster, aka Toddy, stepped carefully over an icy patch on the last step of the stairs and onto the first of the string of docks. She clung to a loose wooden railing. The last time she'd ventured down the rickety steps onto the half-sunken docks of Grouchy's Marina, she had been holding Big Red's arm. She looked up. A man was staring at her.

"You sure you're in the right place, darlin'? Last time something lovely as you come down here was, oh, about the turn of the century. Why not come in and warm up a bit?" The man threw on a stylish, faux fur, knee-length winter coat and stepped out of the Puss E, a sagging aluminum-sided houseboat. Toddy looked through the picture window behind him. Hanging on the wall over a giant couch, illuminated by a blue light, was what looked like a cheap velvet painting of a nude woman.

"Thank you, but I'm looking for Webb Jackson."

"On *Cirrhosis*. Way down the end."

"Thank you. I've been there before." Toddy kept walking.

The man nodded and winked at her. "Ah, right. Got it now. Yeah, gotcha fine. You was with Big Red, night of the blizzard. Right? Word gets around the docks pretty quick down here." The man shook his head. "That Red . . . he is something, ain't he?"

"Red passed away. Apparently, that didn't get around. And it wasn't what you think."

"Aw, geez. Didn't hear 'bout that."

"Seems word gets around for some things and not for others."

"Well, if Webb don't suit your needs..."

"It has nothing to do with Webb. It's something Red left aboard that should belong with his family. I'm just picking it up."

Toddy continued to carefully work her way down the docks, passing some of the other decrepit patched-up houseboats along the way. Red had told her of his neighbors: the non-talking hermit nicknamed Meltdown on the *Broken Promise*, a couple of hard-living towboat pilots on the *Tom Thumb* and the *Beaver*, and the over-the-hill playboy she had just met on the *Puss E*. It was not the ideal neighborhood for an attractive young Native American woman to be wandering through alone. There were river rats—the real and humankind—lurking under and on the docks. And ducks, which she knew could scatter loudly as she came upon them. She was tempted to turn around. But that was not Toddy. Last month, with Red in the blizzard, it was he who had wanted to turn around midway, saying the docks were too slippery and he was worried about her falling. And then she did fall, spraining her ankle. Big Red had just picked her up and carried her, bridal-style, the rest of the way, onto the houseboat. The image made her smile. That can never happen again, she thought. Such a rough, tough man on the outside. But inside? Toddy knew better. Maybe better than anyone. That night, snowed in with Red aboard *Cirrhosis* during a freak fall blizzard, she'd gotten him to let down his guard. He'd opened up, just a crack, but enough to let some light in, and she'd seen inside. Captivated by his life story and her glimpse into his soul, she'd tried to unlock his demons, knowing there was truly a good man under them. And she'd begun to make progress, gaining his trust, becoming his only confidante, his best friend, even his soul mate. There was more to Red. So much more. Then, just weeks later, he was gone. It was all unfinished—until Cubby's letter came. Cubby, Red's young friend and roommate on *Cirrhosis,* had written Toddy after Red's death and told her of Red's diary and personal effects that might still be stored in the houseboat's hold. Now, she thought, perhaps the rest of Red's story lay in that no doubt moldy diary tucked away somewhere down in the old houseboat's hold.

Red had lost his beloved houseboat to Webb Jackson in a drunken card game, forcing him to live in the Minnesota Veterans Home. It was where Toddy, his nurse there, first met him. "Flushed out with four aces," he'd told her. "My four aces to Webb's flush. Still not enough, Toddy." She never got all the details of that night. Only that Red, refusing to fold, kept betting everything in his possession, including his Dodge Power Wagon truck and things that weren't yet in his possession: his next two paychecks.

She smelled smoke from a wood stove. Would Webb be aboard? She'd had no luck trying to find his number. How would he greet her, a stranger showing up at his door, looking for something in the hold of what was no longer Red's boat? She thought of what Red would have said: "If you don't ask, the answer's always 'no.'" So she pushed on. A towboat's rumbling engines echoed back to her off the buildings on the other bank of the river. Toddy remembered how Red had told her he could identify which towboat was going by at night just by the sound of the engines. The boat's wake reached her as she spied *Cirrhosis*'s bow, its tilted stovepipe, and Red's worn, hand-painted plywood sign: Cirrhosis of the River— Abandon All Hope Yee Women Who Wants to Enter Here. She shook her head, smiled. Then wiped away a tear.

The snow on the front deck of *Cirrhosis* was beaten down by numerous footprints, and the gate in the middle of the rusty steel railing on the red houseboat's blunt, scow-like steel bow was swung half open. It was as if nothing had changed since she and Red had left that morning following the storm. Toddy stepped aboard, took a deep breath, and knocked on the partially-open storm door, which hung at an odd angle off one of its hinges. No answer. She peered inside through the dirty pilothouse window; in the dim light she could see very little. She knocked again, harder. Then went in. Not much had changed, including, unfortunately, the old, stained couch. "Plop yourself down right there and make yourself at home," Red had said last time, before seeing her looking at the couch with suspicion. "Don't worry; nothin's gonna bite you, Toddy," he'd said. "Them bugs that live in that thing always go south for the winter."

Toddy looked aft. "Hello? Webb?" No answer. The faint hissing of the woodstove was the only sound, save for the grinding of the houseboat's steel hull as it rocked and rubbed against the river ice in what remained of the passing towboat's wake. It was getting dark. She searched for a light switch, but first encountered a large flashlight. She scanned the walls and found a switch that turned on a dim Grain Belt Beer sign, but it was enough. She got down on her knees on the worn brown shag carpeting, felt around and located the spring-loaded latch and lifting ring that she knew would let her open the hatch to the hold. Still kneeling, she tried to lift the hatch. It was too heavy for her. Red had done it last time, the night they came back to get the remainder of his things. Easy for him. She stood and bent over the hatch, trying a different approach with better leverage, finally wrestling it open and lifting it back on its hinges until it was upright and leaning slightly against the couch. Shining her light in the hold, she scanned the chamber, spying several cardboard boxes, then sat on the edge of the opening and slid down, landing on the boat's steel bottom. There was no headroom, so she kneeled and reached for the first box, at the same time trying not to think about rats. She found what looked like the diary on the first try, pulling it out, shining the light on a moldy, black-bound book. She opened it to the first page, which read: Orca Bates Diary—Keep the Hell Out, then tucked it under her coat.

At the same time, just outside the marina docks, Skip Dodson, pilot on the towboat *Bull Durham*, was running light and hard, pushing no barges but a lot of water off his blunt bow. The big wake lifted some soft ice flows with seemingly little effort as it rolled its way toward the marina and shore. It reached *Cirrhosis* and lifted it and the docks with a groan. Inside *Cirrhosis*, Toddy felt it first hit the steel houseboat's side and then lift the steel bottom. She moved to climb out of the hold, but never made it, as the rocking caused the big hatch to fall and slam shut, the spring-loaded latch locking. She pushed on it, put her shoulder to it, yelled help! until she was hoarse, and tried not to panic. Finally, resigned to waiting, she pulled her coat tighter, turned off the light to save the battery, and started to say a Native American prayer:

"Wakan Tanka, Great Mystery,
teach me how to trust
my heart,
my mind,
my intuition,
my inner knowing,
the senses of my body . . .

Then she stopped, shook her head, and said, 'Jesus, Wihopa, just don't freak out, okay?' That made her feel better.

Hours went by. Shivering, Toddy eventually nodded off, trapped in a tomb of total darkness, wrapped in her jacket.

The shaky docks began to rock again around midnight from two men who were moving slowly toward *Cirrhosis*, returning from the Slough River Bar.

"Man, this is good stuff you got here, Webb. That Jack Daniels tonight, topped off with this weed of yours, is sending me to somewhere strange, I do believe." Retch stumbled on a loose plank on the dock, caught himself, then gave a wheezy laugh. "Hell, guess I will buy an ounce off you."

"Yeah, it got the power of hash oil, don't it? Almost like tripping."

Retch put the joint in his roach clip and sucked the life out of what was left. The glow was enough to illuminate a long, faded scar that ran diagonally down his left cheek. He threw the remains of the joint into the half-frozen river.

"Where's that big bag of M&Ms you had, Webb? I got me the munchies. Hey, you got food and maybe some beer on the boat? I'll pick up that ounce too . . . if you lend me the money."

Webb stopped and stared at him. "Let me get this straight: You want my money so as you can use it to buy something from me? That right? You are one fucking mooch, Retch, you know that?"

"You know I been broke lately. Bitch ex of mine been taking everything but my shit. I swear I'm gonna get even. And hell, Webb, this would only be one of them short-term loans."

"Retch, I'll give you money, but I'll never lend you any. And keep your eyes on the dock ahead or you'll be in that frozen muddy Miss mush before you knows it."

"Hey, speaking of eyes, I seen that barmaid Lynnette's on you at the Slough tonight, Webb. Yes, sir, I seen that for sure. Might go for some of that myself."

"High mileage, Retch. She got real high mileage. Them's whiskey goggles you been looking through tonight. Too much booze makes everybody look good. Even you and Lynnette."

Retch put Webb's M&Ms in his coat pocket. "Speaking of looking good, you hear about the new lady bridge tender that's coming to run Omaha Railroad Bridge? She's getting transferred from some bridge down south and coming up here. Word has it she wears bib overalls with nothing under the bib. How we gonna run big tows through that narrow Omaha bridge span with that distraction?"

"You don't set up for it right as it is, Retch, even without some pretty woman up there. You best keep your eyes on the river, get your line-up right or you'll take out a few yards of piling and track someday; lose your license."

"Big Red used to run that span blind, remember? Piles of grain barge covers stacked up, blocking his vision so he couldn't see nothing. Hell, he didn't even put a deckhand with a radio on the lead barge to tell him if his line-up was off. Fuck, man, he just knew it. Just knew it. And running Monkey Rudder Bend? Hell, I never seen a guy..."

"Well, Red is Red, Retch. Or was. Anyway, come on aboard. I'll get you that weed. Then I'll give you money so as you can buy it from me. Then maybe I'll rustle up a moldy bag of Cheetos for you to munch on."

Webb reached for the switch on the Grain Belt Beer sign inside the front door, slowly realizing that it was already on. "Huh," he said. "Swore I shut that off when we..." He shook his head. "Man, this weed..."

Retch dropped down onto the couch, then kicked off his work boots. The sound awakened Toddy, who pounded on the floor above her.

Webb and Retch stared at each other, then looked down at the brown shag carpeting. The pounding started again.

Retch shook his head, got up quickly and backed toward the houseboat's front door, shaking his head. "We're some fucked up, man."

"Open the hatch, Retch."

"No fucking way. It's your boat. Your ghost, too."

Webb lifted the hatch very slowly. A light shone up at him, blinding him. He dropped the hatch, backed over by Retch, and the two stood there, staring, until Toddy yelled "help! help!"

"You got a woman in your hold. Or a mermaid. Or something, Webb."

"No shit, Sherlock."

Webb went back to the hatch, bent over, and slowly opened it again. Toddy turned off her flashlight and stood up in the opening, chest high in the hold.

"Jesus, H. Will ya look at that! Never thought old *Cirrhosis* had it in her. If you ain't the prettiest thing to ever come out of a hold."

"You must be Webb," Toddy said, looking up at him.

"Little lady, you got to say something real quick that makes some sense."

"I'm Wihopa Webster. A friend of Orca's . . . ah, Red's. I was his nurse in the Veterans Home. I learned he left some of his personal things behind after you took over ownership of *Cirrhosis*, and I came to get them, that's all. I waited. The door was open. So, I came in. Waited some more. Then I just thought I'd try to find his things in the hold. Then the hatch dropped on me. I just waited down there. Couldn't get out."

"Red's dead."

"I know."

"So, why's his stuff suddenly your stuff?"

"I . . . I just felt, well, Cubby, you see . . ."

"Who the hell's Cubby?"

"He's . . . was . . . kind of a relative, more like a son, really, to Red, and he told me Red left some things."

"So you broke into my boat. Into my house."

"I didn't break in."

Retch moved closer to Toddy, who was still standing in the hold, and leaned down to get a closer look at her. The smell of sweat, M&Ms, whiskey, and stale cigarette smoke filled the damp air in the narrow space between them. Toddy saw the scar that curved across his cheek and down to the corner of his mouth and remembered. So did Retch.

"I know you," Retch said. "You're Red's girl. You was with me on the *Elsie Mae* when Red drove Monkey Rudder Bend back in November."

"I'm not his *girl*. I was his nurse. And friend."

"You had his head messed up pretty bad, as I recall. He weren't himself. Spewing all this liberal shit. No, he weren't the same. Like he were under some spell—some kind of powwow magic. Me and him almost got to fighting about it. Right there in the pilothouse. Me and Red was never like that before."

Webb stepped forward. "Okay, cool it, Retch." Then Webb reached out his hand. "Let me help you out of there, little lady."

"I'm fine," Toddy said, and lifted herself out of the hold. "Please, I should be going."

Retch backed up, blocking the front door. "Why don't you come over and say pretty please?"

"They'll be expecting me back. I really need . . ."

"So how we going to settle this then?" Webb interrupted. "I found an intruder in my house, rifling through my possessions, and now I let her go? Hell, you may have some of my things on you right now. How'd you know what is mine and what was Red's down there in the hold, huh? No, I think you got to calm down, smoke a little weed with us, and iron this out."

"Kind of like a peace pipe. Like your people do," Retch snickered. He reached his right hand behind his back, felt for the door bolt, and locked the door.

"I don't think . . ."

"At least take off that coat so we can see what's under it. You know, see that you don't got nothing of mine."

Toddy was running out of options so she took off the coat, trying to hold the diary against the inside lining as she did so. But it fell to the ground.

"Well, well. Now there's somethin' right away," Webb said, looking down at the floor.

"It's just Red's diary. Personal to him. I wanted to retrieve it. That's all."

They both stared at Toddy. Retch was looking straight at her breasts. She wished she hadn't worn such a tight-fitting sweater that day. Retch reached into his coat pocket. Toddy backed up, which only put her closer to Webb. Then Retch pulled out his package of M&Ms, poured some in his mouth, spilled a few into his right hand, and stepped toward Toddy. He held out his hand.

"Here you go," he said. "Take a green one; they say those green ones makes you real horny."

Toddy froze.

Then she thought of Red. Of something he told her. Because he was always trying to protect her. Needlessly obsessed with that, it seemed back then. But now? Maybe he'd been right. She remembered what he'd said.

Retch moved even closer. She looked up at the tall, lanky man who towered over her.

"You're looking at that scar on me, ain't you, pretty lady?"

Toddy shook her head.

"Know how I got that? Know how I got this long, ugly scar?" Toddy shook her head.

"Street fight years ago. In North Minneapolis. Know who did it?"

Toddy shook her head.

"An Indian. A fucking Indian did it."

Retch lifted his right arm and began to reach toward Toddy.

Red's voice was strong in her head now: You ever get cornered, promise me this Toddy: don't ever try to rationalize nothing. That's why good people gets themselves killed. They don't believe evil when it's right in front of them, staring them in the face. But evil's everywhere. So don't think. And don't telegraph. Don't look for the door. Don't look like you're about to run. Put your hands at your sides. Don't telegraph nothing. Then, real sudden like, take your right or left arm, whichever is stronger, and lift it fast and straight and HARD, palm up, straight up, right under the nose of that monster who's in your face. He'll never see it coming. He'll be on his knees and seeing stars before you even turn to run. And then run, Toddy. Run like you never run before.

So that's what Toddy did.

And as Retch crumpled to the floor, she picked up the diary, unbolted the door, and ran. Webb, in pursuit, but fifty pounds overweight, never had a chance.

It was an escape of sorts, at least that night. But Toddy knew she'd be looking over her shoulder for a long time.

The End of the Line

SIT DOWN, POP

Everyone showed up right on time that cold (-7 degrees F) January day at Pickering Wharf in Salem, Massachusetts. All eight men were there for the First Annual Middle-Aged Men Tell Sea Stories in the Cabin of a Frozen Sailboat in the Middle of the Winter luncheon. I'd arrived early, opened the cockpit tarp a bit to allow entry for the expected guests, heated *Elsa's* frozen cabin to a relatively pleasant 60 degrees, and laid out snacks, lunch, and liquid sea-story-rendering supplies (rum).

The cast of characters ranged in age from 38 to 88. The 88-year-old was Grampy, my dad, who perhaps doesn't qualify as middle-aged, but I figured we needed the wisdom of time on our side. Boats owned over the lifetimes of the eight numbered over 30, both sail and power, wooden, fiberglass, and steel, from 22- to 42-feet. Professions of the storytellers included CEO, psychologist, boat builder, golf equipment salesman, English teacher, Web designer, and shoe machinery equipment salesman. There was one great grandfather, a couple of grandfathers, fathers of kids five to 28, and one with his first baby on the way. Everyone, I knew, had faced their share of life's stresses: teenage parenting horror stories, job losses, and cancer and other health crises, and everyone seemed more than ready for this sojourn from reality. (I know they were ready because every one of them showed up for the noon luncheon, arriving in the four minutes between 11:58 and 12:02.)

It wasn't long until the stories flowed.

The first one was a bit of a coincidence. We got to talking about Seal Bay, a wonderful spot tucked away inside a part of Vinalhaven island, Maine. I mentioned how, several years ago, my son Nick (aged 15 at the time) and I had re-supplied *Chang Ho*, my old Cape Dory 25, in Stonington, sailed across East Penobscot Bay, and found our favorite 10-foot spot way up in Seal Bay. We figured this would be a fun and deserted spot to just hang out for a couple of days, eat all our new supplies, do some varnishing and dinghy sailing, and see if I couldn't finally win a game of cribbage. We ended up laying there for two days and nights in the grip of a nor'easter. It came out of nowhere, and it blew like stink, probably 35 knots, cold and with driving rain. Thank God for my little cabin heater. One other boat came in after us and spent two days setting and resetting its anchor upwind of us; they were the only thing that worried me. As for us, we were protected, and my 25-pound plow was set well. We went through most of our supplies (including Nick's treasured Jiffy Pop popcorn), Nick finished all his summer reading, and I lost every cribbage game but one. But we were cozy with our polar fleece sleeping bags in that tiny cabin of our tiny boat. As we yawed back and forth with each gust, I mostly thought of what it must have been like offshore. That's when I shivered.

My brother Chris nodded his head knowingly as I said this. "I know," he said. "Dad and I were in it!"

"I'll never forget," he said, "it was mid-July 2000, and, unlike you and Nick, we didn't stay put. In fact, before we left for Allen Island, we'd spent the night not two miles from where you guys were, in Perry Creek."

"Well, you have the cabin sole (floor) on this one; this story is all yours," I said. Brother Chris took it from there, recounting the story of their adventure on *Scarabee*, his Luders 33 sloop.

Sit Down, Pop

"I figured we still had a nice weather window to make it west on a leg back toward Marblehead from Vinalhaven, maybe to Allen or Burnt Island just south of Port Clyde, which would be a good stop and keep us out on our rhumb line for the next day. The wind was then south/southeast at about 10 knots, and we had a good sail from Perry Creek. It was smooth enough for Dad to steer, but I still worried a lot about my octogenarian father when he moved around. He was shaky on his feet, and throughout our cruise he kept standing up to look around. It made me nervous when it was anything but flat calm. "Sit down, Pop," I kept saying; almost completely deaf, he usually didn't hear me and kept standing. I couldn't blame him; he's always loved cruising and has cruised Maine for sixty years.

"Anyway, at day's end I dropped the 25-pound Danforth in the bight at the northeast end of Allen Island. I had to anchor very close to shore to find water that was shallow enough and still let out a necessary 100′ of scope in 19 feet of depth. It had been a long sail, and it felt good to get the hook set, though I was nervous being that close to shore, knowing if we dragged even a little we'd be on the rocks. We had dinner below, but I popped my head up frequently, even though the wind was still light and from the south. Though I still hadn't heard a forecast for any wind shift, I knew I wasn't going to sleep well that night. Then, right around sunset, when then wind usually dies, it strengthened and shifted to the northeast. Suddenly we were anchored 50 feet off what was now a lee shore. I knew we had to get out of there, and we upped anchor. I thought of running for it and trying to make Boothbay at night, but Muscongus Bay is no place to be with no visibility, as anyone who has sailed there knows. So, we headed for the other side of Allen Island, where I'd be protected from the northeast wind. At 2030 hours I successfully re-anchored. There was a false sense of calm here due to the height of the island we were under. Still, I slept with one eye open.

"The wind was still northeasterly at dawn, and though the weather reported high winds it didn't seem too strong because of our high windward shore (Allen is 134 feet high in places). It all gave me a false sense of confidence, and because of that I made a couple of mistakes: I put up the full main when I should have reefed it, and I didn't immediately stow the Danforth after hauling it up, as I was worried about Dad at the wheel and hurried back aft. It was relatively calm in the lee as we motored along Allen Island on a southwesterly course that would take us out clear of the ledges, shoals and small islands until I could head more west towards Pemaquid Point. Unfortunately, I forgot about the anchor and its pile of line on the bow until we cleared the island and picked up the full impact of the wind (35 knots) and seas (10-foot rollers). Now I had a dilemma. I envisioned the anchor and its rode sliding overboard in the rapidly building seas and getting tangled up in the prop and rudder. And yet I didn't dare leave my 84-year-old father at the wheel while going forward to retrieve it. I also didn't dare turn in these seas for fear of jeopardizing the anchor even more as we rolled. Something had to be done.

'Do you think you can steer and stand up OK, Pop?' I asked.

'Say again?' he replied.

'ARE YOU OK STEERING?' I yelled.

'Oh, sure. Good fun,' he said, smiling, as he pulled himself upright on the binnacle bar. 'And where are you going?' he asked, almost casually.

'NEVER MIND. JUST STEER FOR THAT SMALL ISLAND!' I shouted.

"I crawled forward and, on one occasion, felt suspended in air as the *Scarabee* fell off a wave. Ungracefully, I threw myself onto the pile of anchor and rode and bundled it all up as best I could, tying the whole pile to the big bow cleat. Then I crawled back aft.

"We were now on a sleigh ride, with a 35-knot northeast wind on our quarter and big rolling seas. Visibility was very poor in the gloom of fog and emerging rain. Despite it all, we were doing ok, and I was confident of our position in the ledge-filled Muscongus Bay. I had great faith in my programmed GPS map as it glowed in front of me next to the compass, magically leading the way as I steered along the electronic line on the screen. Only two things really worried me: One was that the 30-year-old steering cable would part. I was now steering using both hands, spinning the wheel lock to lock, trying to keep from broaching, and I keep thinking about the strain on the cable, pulleys, and clamps below me. I also worried about Dad, who kept standing up to look around. 'Good fun,' he kept saying, like a kid on his first carnival ride. 'Sit down, Pop,' I kept yelling in reply.

"Well, I thought, just keep sailing on this course 'round Pemaquid Point, and follow the next electronic line on the GPS into Boothbay. Then some peace, maybe beat Dad in cribbage, have a stiff cocktail, and a nice sleep.

I glanced down at the GPS map, but this time what I saw ahead of me on the screen looked like the edge of the earth, a grey mass of slashes indicating the end of this chart chip's coverage. The next electronic chart, a matchbook-sized black piece of plastic and silicone, was somewhere below deck in a box above the starboard bunk. There was absolutely no way I could leave the wheel to find it. And there was no way Dad was going to try to stand here and steer in these seas. I had no choice but to send Dad below to find it.

'DAD,' I yelled, 'WE NEED ANOTHER CHART CHIP!'

'What kind of chips do you want?' he asked.

'NO, NO, FOR THE GPS, WE NEED A NEW CHART CHIP.'

'Say again?'

"We were going nowhere fast. Dad tried to stand up.

'SIT DOWN, POP!' He sat down. 'LOOK, DAD, WORK YOUR WAY BELOW AND LOOK FOR A SMALL BOX OVER THE STARBOARD BUNK THAT SAYS GARMIN ON IT AND BRING IT TO ME. AND HANG ON ALL THE TIME.'

"Dad came through. Somehow he made it down the ladder, worked his way to the bunk shelf, found the box, and came back up without falling.

"I put the new chart chip in.

"We made Boothbay fine later that day.

"And that night, Dad even beat me at cribbage.

'All good fun,' he said as he worked his way forward to his bunk.

And not a bad day's work for an 84-year-old.

THE TIDE WAITS FOR NO MAN

In the 12th century, King Canute set his throne by the seashore. A tiny wave rushed up the sand and lapped at his feet. "How dare you!" the English king shouted. "Ocean, turn back now! I have ordered you to retreat before me, and now you must obey."

Nice try, Your Highness.

Our oceans aren't turning back. That's clearer than ever, especially during our recent devastatingly high tides. That got me to thinking about old King Canute. I regularly walk by Brown's Island, a lovely spot off Marblehead, only accessible at low tide by foot. Yesterday, I was walking this route about an hour after low tide. I knew from forty years of watching from shore as well as anchoring behind the island at high water that access to the island on foot would end soon. So, I was surprised to see a young couple cross the rapidly disappearing small piece of mudflat and head out to the island. They crossed, walked up and down the beach, then headed into the woods to explore. It being winter, I was sure that nine or so hours marooned on the island was not their intention. I watched, hoping they'd come out of the woods very soon. Didn't happen. I continued my walk along the shore, occasionally looking over my shoulder for the couple's emergence. I walked for another fifteen minutes and returned, heading back to my car. As I approached, I saw the couple finally appear from the woods, seemingly without a care in the world. Again, they walked up and down the beach, arm-in-arm, stopping occasionally to pick up and examine stones. Not sure whether to be amused or worried, I waited for them to look toward shore.

Finally, seemingly lost in each other's gaze, they meandered down the beach to the point where they had crossed over to the island on the mudflat. Then they looked up. That's odd. No mudflat—only a world filled in by the Atlantic Ocean. I've seen folks trapped by the tide before. In almost every case, people act like dogs, walking back and forth along the water's edge (as if that will make any difference!) and then, with a shrug of finality that comes with the realization that (a) they're devoid of options, and (b) the water's only going to get deeper, they simply step into the water and slog to shore, no doubt mindful of tides forevermore. And that's what this couple did. All things considered, this couple's journey had a happy ending.

As I drove home, I thought of another ending. It's from "The Ledge," one of the most heartbreaking short stories I've ever read. A fisherman, his young teenage son, his teen nephew, and their dog all go hunting for sea ducks early one Christmas morning. They take their lobster boat and skiff out to a tiny ledge, Devil's Hump, near Brown Cow Island, on the Maine coast. They arrive midway through an incoming tide so they can land on the ledge, set up and have plenty of time for shooting. The fisherman knows what he's doing. They will have about three hours before the ledge is completely submerged by the next high tide. He anchors the lobster boat a hundred yards offshore. They take the skiff in, slide it up the sloping rocks, set up for shooting, and become immersed in their duck hunting from the top of the ledge. They shoot some birds. The dog fetches some. The fisherman takes the skiff occasionally to pick up the birds the dog doesn't get, returns, and pulls the skiff up on the ledge. He does this several times, but the last time the skiff isn't pulled up far enough. The rising tide gets the better of the small boat; perhaps it's lifted by a surge. It drifts away. The fisherman is the first to notice. His stark realization, as quoted from the story:

> [He] was unprepared for the sudden blaze that flashed upward inside him from belly to head. He was standing looking at the shelf where the skiff was . . . . He gaped, seeing nothing but the flat shelf of rock. He whirled, started toward the boys, slipped, recovered himself, fetched a complete circle, and stared at the unimaginably empty shelf. Its emptiness made him feel as if everything he had done that day so far, his life so far, he had dreamed."

They're stranded; instinctively, they move away from the sea to the ledge's highest point. They shoot their guns to try to attract attention, but there's no one around. The encroaching tide of the cold, deep blue Atlantic, steadfast as always, seems to hunger for these alien creatures who cower just out of its reach. Slowly, almost imperceptibly, it climbs the seaweed covered grey-black ledge, breaking into foam just out of reach of those huddling at the top. It keeps coming. The dog swims away. Drowns. It begins to snow. Then darken. The space left on the remaining piece gets smaller and smaller, until it's nothing at all. The nephew disappears in the whiteness and the sea. The fisherman jams his feet into a crevice in the rock and tells his son to climb on his shoulders. The ledge is gone now. The tide keeps coming. The fisherman loses all feeling in his legs but continues to stand, stalwart against the tide, as if commanding its cessation. But the tide, as it did with King Canute, acts the way it always has.

And the cycle of life goes on.

SEVEN BLOCKS OF WOOD

During the three years my elderly dad cared for my bedridden mom at home, he was pretty much housebound. So, he thought, "I'll make a model of *Phyllis*, the family boat, the boat we spent our honeymoon on over fifty years ago, the boat the three boys were raised on, the boat we learned a lot about life on." It didn't matter that he hadn't built an intricate model boat before. He just began with seven blocks of wood and, like life, worked his way through it. It gave him purpose at a time when his one care, my mom, was at the end of the line. While he shaped and hollowed out the hull and built from scratch every piece—down to the tiny red towels monogramed with 'Phyllis'—his memories of life on the real *Phyllis* floated back. I remember my first time going down to his basement workshop and watching him, an eighty-five-year-old still focused on building something, and doing so with care. "How are you going to make a model of a fully-rigged sailboat from a pile of scrap pine boards, Dad?" He just winked at me. "It'll take forever, even if you figure out how to do it," I added. He just smiled.

Somehow, in the end, he had perfectly hand-fashioned every part: a miniature anchor, tiny clock and barometer, coal stove, winches and rigging, and a forward hatch. "You went aboard through that hatch in August of 1950 as a newborn, wedged into the forepeak in a basket," he said. "You may not remember. But I do." His attachment, and now mine, to *Phyllis*, I don't question.

Dad had learned the ropes of life by then. Part of that, I guess, was not letting go of what is good and true but rather celebrating those things by continuing to build something, and in so doing rekindling and creating more memories, including this one for me: that of an elderly dad and his middle-aged son standing shoulder to shoulder in a basement workshop, each temporarily forgetting the knots of their lives, each drifting back in time, while they built something new. It was bit by bit, tiny piece by tiny piece, as the model took shape, that we shared who we really were. For a time, and sometimes for all their time, fathers and sons hold much back from each other, perhaps out of fear, perhaps out of pride, perhaps out of cowardice or shame. But always there comes a point when the sands of time have almost drained from the glass, when there's little chance left to share what really matters, and, like the lines of a well-drawn hull, what is really true.

TILTING AT WINDMILLS

Four days were spent in thinking what name to give him, because (as he said to himself) it was not right that a horse belonging to a knight so famous, and one with such merits of his own, should be without some distinctive name, and he strove to adapt it so as to indicate what he had been before belonging to a knight-errant, and what he then was.

Cervantes describing Don Quixote's careful naming of Rocinante, his steed

For a few moments, let your mind be not a steed, but a gliding bird, a thoughtful soaring bird flying over a harbor chock full of boats of all types and sizes. You've been away for a generation or two, and now you're coming back. You're full of anticipation and yearning for the place you left behind. You begin your flight at the harbor's mouth, where the biggest boats are tethered in this great 2000-boat anchorage. You look down. Then you swoop closer, skimming the tops of the masts of some of the sailboats. They're aluminum now, these masts. Not the tall spruce ones of days of yore. As you soar by, the early morning breeze makes the halyards clink rather than thump, as they had on the wooden masts of the olden days when you flew here. You cock your head and listen. It's a different sound. Maybe better, maybe not—depends who you are and where you come from, you think. Like the wooden mast to the aluminum one, that sound has evolved over time. Now it's a common sound representative of what's new down there, and maybe it's enjoyed by some, maybe not; maybe it's an acquired taste, you think. You keep flying and looking. There are fewer of them today, these boats with masts, replaced by so many other types of motorized craft. And the wooden boats are mostly gone; many have evolved into sleek, two- and three-outboard fiberglass center consoles. When you last flew over, years ago, a big outboard was 28 horsepower; now it's 350. The world changes for lots of reasons, you think. Maybe for the good. Maybe not. Depends on who you are and where you come from. You keep flying. You go down lower. The harbor's a mile long and a half-mile wide, and the boats are getting smaller as you reach the shallow end at the head. Come on, you think, go down a bit more. It's okay; the masts are getting shorter as the sailboats get smaller.

There! What's that down there, between that large powerboat and those two center console outboards? Wow, you think. I bet those boats, those in their prime, those sleek ones with the 350-horsepower outboards, I bet they get there fast, wherever they're going. And I bet the kids love the speed and thrill of it all. But this little boat, between them, almost unnoticeable, the one partially rebuilt and with no mast yet in it, she sits like a bird perfectly alighted on the water, perfectly acclimated to her environment. You circle around, going lower and lower, until your own wing tips momentarily eclipse the glint from the sun's morning rays on the water. Wait, there's a man there, sticking his head out of the tiny cabin; he seems content, snug in his own era. He must have been sleeping aboard. He's a white-haired man, fit-looking though way past his prime, probably pushing 80. His vessel, too, may be pushing 80, a craft from a bygone day no doubt, and obviously amid a careful, loving rebuild. There's only one primer coat of paint on the hull, and some pieces of the boat are missing: part of the cockpit, a piece of the rail, the companionway hatch. And of course, the mast isn't there. But you can just tell, by her narrow beam, her lovely sheer, and her sleek, double-ended lines, that this is a thoroughbred. You know now, as you swoop very close, that this is the former steed of a knight-errant. This is a *Rozinante*, a legendary design from legendary designer L. Francis Herreshoff. This is one of the finest sailboats ever designed. Ever.

The world keeps changing, but this man down there seems to have hung onto the past. Maybe he knows something. Maybe he hasn't forgotten something. Perhaps he knows enough about what's good about the past that he's going to hang on to just that. Perhaps he has an inherent sense of quality and knows he's found it right here in this boat. The fast boats, those sleek, modern, high-powered ones all around him, are what much of the world seems to want now. Whenever their people get aboard, wherever they're going, wherever there is, they want to get there quicker. As you tilt your wings and begin your ascent, taking one last glimpse at the white-haired fellow and the beloved boat below, you think: yet that man, when he gets aboard, is already there!

SOME OLD LOVE SONG

The Dutchman's not the kind of man
To keep his thumb jammed in the dam
That holds his dreams in
But that's a secret only Margaret knows
When Amsterdam is golden in the morning
Margaret brings him breakfast
She believes him
He thinks the tulips bloom beneath the snow
He's mad as he can be, but Margaret only sees that sometimes
Sometimes she sees her unborn children in his eyes

              Michael Smith

As I head up the hill to the small seaside home of two old friends, the lyrics from this moving song stream out the open windows and drift down to me. I stand outside for a moment and listen while looking back out to sea. Then I open the door and step into the living room/kitchen, where perhaps a dozen 60- to 80-year-old men are scattered around, singing intently to the music of a fiddle and two guitars. A few nod and smile as I take the last seat on the couch and pick up the chorus with the others:

Let us go to the banks of the ocean
Where the walls rise above the Zuider Zee

Long ago I used to be a young man
And dear Margaret remembers that for me

There are no young men in the room, only older men of boats and the sea. Disheveled, not fancy, they too are not inclined to hold their dreams in. For them, dreams have long ago been realized, or perhaps not yet attained—or perhaps not ready to be abandoned. But all of them, in this old house by the sea, look back, perhaps at what they lived for and what they'll leave behind. I look around: There's my old fiddler friend who's had a couple of heart attacks and fainting spells but still rides his only vehicle, a motorcycle, year-round; there's another talented musician, a performer and boatyard worker whose rapidly advancing cancer has allowed him to look into the abyss as he told me that night; there's a veteran offshore fisherman who has recently lost his son to the sea.

And together they sing. The words resonate; tears fill hardened, wind-worn eyes.

The Dutchman still wears wooden shoes
His cap and coat are patched with love
That Margaret sewed in
Sometimes he thinks he's still in Rotterdam
He watches tugboats down canals
And calls out to them when he thinks he knows the captain
'Til Margaret comes to take him home again
Through unforgiving streets that trip him
Though she holds his arm
Sometimes he thinks that he's alone and calls her name

As I sing along in my place on the end of the couch by the door, I think of my Margaret and of other Margarets in the world and how blessed those of us are who have one. Like the boats and the ocean that we call she, they cradle us, buoy us up, carry us along. Sometimes they take us away to far-off places, and sometimes they take us away forever. Maybe what these men are feeling is that what they've lived for is to be loved, and they don't want that to stop. And on they sing together.

The windmills whirl the winter in
She winds his muffler tighter
They sit in the kitchen
Some tea with whiskey keeps away the dew
He sees her for a moment calls her name
She makes the bed up humming some old love song
She learned it when the tune was very new
He hums a line or two
They hum together in the night
The Dutchman falls asleep and Margaret blows the candle out
Long ago I used to be a young man
And dear Margaret remembers that for me

POLYSULFIDE

In August 2011, a man named Martin turned 60. When his big day came, he went to the far southeast end of a parking lot by a police station and put a bullet in his head. He wasn't ill. He wasn't depressed. He'd suffered no lost loves or loved ones. He had all his faculties. He had neither financial nor legal problems. Martin just didn't believe in his future, and living in the present or back through the past wasn't enough. And so he planned his death, down to the last detail, complete with a My Life and Death website that was scheduled to go live the moment he was dead. Martin feared old age, dementia, irrelevancy. He feared loss of dignity. And so he got out while the getting was good. His website explains:

> I've run the race. I already got to the finish line. I didn't croak on the way. I didn't get embarrassed. I didn't break a leg. I sprinted most of the time and sometimes I slowed to a walk to catch my breath. But I could see the finish line and I liked it!! The last thing on Earth I was going to do when I got there [Where is there? Heaven?] was... keep going. I completed the race because I went over every hurdle that was in my way. Sometimes I fell. But I got back up and ran that much harder.

Someday, I would fall down the stairs or slip in the bathtub or get caught walking in a never-ending circle or driving to the store only to end up in Maine. And nobody would know the difference—at least for a while.

I didn't want to put Super Glue in my eyes thinking it was eye drops because I suffer from dementia. I didn't want to exist being unable to type on a keyboard because of Parkinson's or drive a car or recognize the people I love. I didn't want to be beaten to death by an intruder or eaten alive by maggots. If you thought I was going to drift through this type of embarrassment and indignity, you were wrong!

And, here's the clincher . . . it's only going to get worse!

I've been to the penthouse. It may only be a 10-story building, but I refuse to ride the elevator down to the basement! Nope, I'm going out on top. The rest of you can go out whenever you want.

 The problem is, Martin didn't really finish the race. Martin made his own finish line. He moved it up. He bet against himself. He couldn't imagine any value in getting older, couldn't imagine any further beauty or grace that could still come his way. Perhaps he just didn't care anymore. Or didn't have anyone to care about.

 Satchel Paige said, "Age is a question of mind over matter. If you don't mind, it doesn't matter." How true.

 This story isn't about Martin. It's about someone who didn't mind, someone to whom age didn't matter. It's about someone who got out at age 93, rather than 60. Yes, he fell, he choked, he drooled, he ate moldy food, he totaled his car. He got old. But he'd learned the ropes. He cared about his life. All of it.

From the moment we're born, we're learning the ropes. We're an open book, a tiny baby, completely vulnerable to everything, with no control over anything, no prejudices toward good or evil, and no plan whatsoever, except to scream for food. I probably screamed for food. You, too. Someone must have been good enough to pick us up, maybe to stop our screaming. Someone must have cared. Caring right to the end, I think, should be our number one job.

From the moment we're born, we're also running out of time, getting ever closer to the end of the line. Whether we care or not, the ropes of our lives are full of Gordian knots, stomach knots, relationship, love and marriage knots, job and boss knots, ethical knots, and a seemingly endless string of tangles and bends.

There's a lot to learn from the end of the line, such as from this 93-year-old. My dad. Still smiling after all those years.

∞

There in front of us was *Phyllis*. Looking ashamed of her condition and very much out of her element, she sat uncovered under some pines in a field behind a barn, her old, rotted mast lying beside her. I stepped back a bit, feeling that our very presence must be embarrassing to her. I hadn't wanted to return to *Phyllis* in the first place, knowing what we would find in a boat born sixty years ago and long gone from our family care. It was Dad's idea, coming back to see how she'd fared after all these years.

I glanced over at my father. He was smiling, moving forward, intently curious. One eye drooped a bit, a remnant of a couple of strokes he'd had nearly a decade before. His old pea green jacket, faded and ripped at the pockets, clashed with his blue tweed hat, which sat askew on the back of his head. I'd long ago given up suggesting how he might improve his attire. When I'd made suggestions, he'd simply smiled and said with certainty: "Nope. That's not what it's about, Dave."

What is it all about, I wondered now? I'd been wanting to ask him that for a long time, figuring someone of his age and wisdom, someone who was still smiling after all these years, would surely have the answer. But somehow, I never could. Maybe I was afraid of the answer. Or afraid that he wouldn't have one. And then what?

I watched as he shuffled still closer to what remained of the old family boat. So little time was left for either of them now. And then I thought of Mom, the love of his life for fifty-five years. She had dropped to eighty-eight pounds after her second stroke. Then came the emphysema. She couldn't breathe at all without her oxygen, so Dad carried around her portable tank in one hand while with the other he struggled with both the plastic air hose and my mother's unsteady step. Taking care of Mom had become his mission. It was just as well, I thought. It filled a space made by the end of so much else. My two brothers and I were long out of his care; the job of raising us was done. Dad's career had ended many years ago. Even his post-retirement yacht club commodore stint had passed. And his tennis and cribbage partners? Most of them were dead. And here he was facing his old beloved boat, which was rotting away in some field away from the sea.

My God, I thought. This is the end of the line, Dad. How can you still be smiling? But, as usual, I just stood there, mute. A damp early spring wind shook *Phyllis'* tarp, and I began to shiver.

Dad bent down and looked carefully at the peeling, rust-streaked hull of his old friend *Phyllis*. "She's still bleeding," he said. "Never could fix that bleeding. Heads were knocked off the galvanized boat nails when she was first built in '39; rust bled out, worked its way to the surface over time." He backed away and slowly straightened, his eyes still focused on the rust on the hull. "Oxidation. You can't stop it. Capillary action of some sort brings the rust to the surface of the wood," he said. As he rubbed a stained section of the old hull, I noticed the blotch marks that advanced age had left on the back of his hand. Then he shook his head slowly. "You can putty it, paint it, treat it any way you want. But you can't stop it." Then he looked down at something purple and yellow at his feet; an early spring crocus had somehow emerged from the winter-ravaged, half-frozen earth. "Like that flower," he said, pointing. "Wonderful about life, isn't it? Time moves things along, no matter what. It's just the way things are."

I looked down at the crocus, just beginning its journey, then over at Dad. An elderly man I thought could never get old now stood beside me, buffeted by the raw March wind. I wanted to speak but couldn't. As always, Dad was so wrapped up in the significance of the immediate moment, it didn't seem right to break his focus.

And so, I looked at *Phyllis*. The beautiful, resilient wooden boat that had sailed our family through calms and storms was now dwindling away. I remember thinking that, given enough time, her timbers would eventually rot right back into the earth, the place from which they had sprung as oak, fir, and mahogany trees more than a half century ago.

"Maybe you should know something," Dad said, looking up at me.

It jolted me, that phrase of his. It seemed so strangely serious, profound and even foreboding, coming from a man who always seemed to operate happily in the moment at hand, whistling his way through life's easy and tough spots. I remember thinking: Perhaps this is the time he's chosen to pass on the baton of his life's wisdom; perhaps the something I should know is how to find happiness in the most dismal of situations; perhaps what is coming are instructive words on how to finally be comfortable with myself and cope with life's all-too-fleeting passage. Or perhaps . . . perhaps he just wants to say a few words about how he feels, deep down, about a certain middle-aged son of his. I turned and gave him my fullest attention, tuning out the sounds of the wind-buffeted tarp, the view of the boat, and the field around us.

"Polysulfide," he said.

"What, Dad?"

"Polysulfide. You should know about that stuff. It might have absorbed the rust. But it hadn't been invented yet. Resilient, long lasting, gives when necessary, but somehow still sticks. Good stuff. DuPont came up with it. Maybe 3M, now that I think about it."

I shook my head and smiled. "Let's go home, Dad." And we trudged away through the remaining patches of snow, both knowing that we'd probably never see *Phyllis* again. Then Dad slowed and turned slightly, his eyes back on his boat.

"Better watch ahead," I said. "Pay attention to this path we're on; it's a slippery one."

"Can you still see it?" he asked.

"See what, Dad?"

"Even with her keel in the grave, it's still there."

"What's still there?" I asked, shivering again and beginning to become frustrated. There was a slight edge to my voice. I looked hard, but all I saw was a neglected old boat, down on her luck and out of her element.

"The grace and dignity. There's still such grace and dignity, despite it all," he said finally.

Grace and dignity, despite it all.

I took Dad's arm and we headed home. Smiling.

Made in United States
North Haven, CT
02 April 2025